HARBINGERS 19

Into the Blue

Angela Hunt

D1522823

Alton Gansky, Bill Myers and Jeff Gerke

Published by Amaris Media International.
Copyright © 2017 Angela Hunt
Cover Design: Angela Hunt
Photo credits: © *MikeDrago.cz* – fotolia.com

All rights reserved. No part of this book may be reproduced, stored in a retrieval system, or transmitted in any form or by any other means—electronic, mechanical, photocopy, recording, or any other—except for brief quotations in printed reviews, without prior permission from the publisher.

ISBN-13: 978-1544742960
ISBN-10: 1544742967

For more information, visit us on Facebook:
https://www.facebook.com/pages/Harbingers/705107309586877

or *www.harbingersseries.com*.

HARBINGERS

A novella series by
Bill Myers, Frank Peretti, Jeff Gerke, Angela Hunt,
and Alton Gansky

In this fast-paced world with all its demands, the five of us wanted to try something new. Instead of the longer novel format, we wanted to write something equally as engaging but that could be read in one or two sittings—on the plane, waiting to pick up the kids from soccer, or as an evening's read.

We also wanted to play. As friends and seasoned novelists, we thought it would be fun to create a game we could participate in together. The rules were simple:

Rule #1
Each of us will write as if we were one of the characters in the series:

Bill Myers will write as Brenda, the street-hustling tattoo artist who sees images of the future.

Frank Peretti will write as the professor, the atheist ex-priest ruled by logic.

Jeff Gerke will write as Chad, the mind reader with devastating good looks and an arrogance to match.

Angela Hunt will write as Andi, the brilliant-but-geeky young woman who sees inexplicable patterns.

Alton Gansky will write as Tank, the naïve, big-hearted jock with a surprising connection to a healing power.

Rule #2

Instead of the five of us writing one novella together (we're friends but not crazy), we would write it like a TV series. There would be an overarching storyline into which we'd plug our individual novellas, with each story written from our character's point of view.

If you're keeping track, this is the order:

Harbingers #1—*The Call*—Bill Myers
Harbingers #2—*The Haunt*ed—Frank Peretti
Harbingers #3—*The Sentinels*—Angela Hunt
Harbingers #4—*The Girl*—Alton Gansky

Volumes #1-4 omnibus: *Cycle One: Invitation*

Harbingers #5—*The Revealing*—Bill Myers
Harbingers #6—*Infestation*—Frank Peretti
Harbingers #7—*Infiltration*—Angela Hunt
Harbingers #8—*The Fog*—Alton Gansky

Volumes #5-8 omnibus: *Cycle Two: Mosaic*

Harbingers #9—*Leviathan*—Bill Myers
Harbingers #10—*The Mind Pirates*—Frank Peretti
Harbingers #11—*Hybrids*—Angela Hunt
Harbingers #12—*The Village*—Alton Gansky

Volumes 9-12 omnibus: *Cycle Three: The Probing*

Harbingers #13—*Piercing the Veil*—Bill Myers
Harbingers #14—*Home Base*—Jeff Gerke
Harbingers #15—*Fairy*—Angela Hunt
Harbingers #16—*At Sea*—Alton Gansky

Volumes 13-16 omnibus: *Cycle Four: The Pursuit*

Harbingers #17—*Piercing the Veil*—Bill Myers
Harbingers #18—*Interesting Times*—Jeff Gerke
Harbingers #19—*Into the Blue*—Angela Hunt

There you have it, at least for now. We hope you'll find these as entertaining in the reading as we are in the writing.

Bill, Frank, Jeff, Angie, and Al

Chapter 1

For about the hundredth time, I stared at the drawing from Brenda's sketchbook: the man wearing a black robe, with dark hair and a beard, floating above snow-covered mountains. Below him, near the yawning entrance of a cave, stood a boy who looked like Daniel. And in the snow, scattered around like cast-off toys, were figures that bore an unwelcome and uncanny resemblance to Tank, Brenda, Chad . . . and me.

"Not going to happen." I shoved the sketch

ANGELA HUNT

beneath several scrawled pages on my dining room table. "Maybe it's a warning, not a prophecy."

Who was it that once asked a similar question? Oh, yeah—Ebenezer Scrooge, when he asked the Spirit of Christmas Future if the things he'd seen were realities or possibilities. In his case, they had been shadows of things that *might* be, and Scrooge had been able to alter the course of his life. But in our case . . .

I lowered my head into my hands, forcing my brain to remember details. Brenda's sketches were usually prophetic, but when we were in the horrible fog around a San Diego high rise, she had drawn Tank with his chest ripped open while some horrible creatures snacked on his internal organs. That scenario didn't happen. We had defeated those monsters, so maybe we could defeat the man in black, too.

Or maybe we should just go back to where we all came from and forget about the last few months— about the Gate, the Watchers, the orbs, the black-eyed kids, the killer fungus, the fog creatures, Littlefoot, and the man being groomed to be the Antichrist candidate for this generation. The Big Bad.

A tempting idea, but could we go back to being the naive people we once were? Could I go back to the university and find a job as a research assistant? What would I list on my resume as my last job? *Ninja warrior against supernatural wickedness? Resister of alien forces intent on world destruction?*

Chad might be able to return to his life as a mind-reader/part-time gambler, but he hadn't been with us long enough to have burned every bridge.

Daniel could never go back to the psychiatric hospital where we'd found him—Brenda would die

2

first. And Brenda had become such a protective and loving mom that little remained of the sardonic tattoo artist who had tatted our images on Tank's oversized arm.

And as for Tank . . . a smile crept onto my lips. The big guy had dropped out of college to join our unique little team. I suppose he could go back to the little town in Oregon where he grew up, and maybe his uncle would give him a job in the sheriff's department. But writing speeding tickets would feel like babysitting kittens compared to fending off flesh-eating fog monsters.

I rubbed my tired eyes and looked around my empty hotel suite. The clock above the microwave said 2:30 a.m., so most of the others were asleep—if they could sleep at all. Tank was probably sleeping like a baby, but I'd bet Brenda and Chad were still fuming about the stunt Tank pulled in Beijing. We had found the antichrist candidate, we had, at great risk, managed to kill him, and then Tank had done what Tank always does. He loved. He healed. He made Ambrosi Giacomo whole.

I blew out a breath and went back to the computer. We had been tracking Giacomo, the Gate's "big bad" for this generation, and our system had worked well enough for us to intercept him at the Temple of Heaven in Beijing. But now the Gate had to be aware that we were onto their plan, so we needed to try a new tactic. But what?

I pressed my hands to my forehead and closed my eyes. For a split second, I wished the professor was with me—he had always been able to remind me of principles I tended to forget—but he was tripping the light fantastic in some other dimension, having left us

3

because he assumed we were capable enough to handle the Gate on our own.

"You shouldn't make assumptions, Professor."

I lifted my head at sudden burst of insight—not from thinking of the professor, but from remembering something Tank often said: *A good defense is great, but a good offense is better.*

We needed to go on the offense. We needed to move the ball into the enemy's part of the court—er, field. We needed to sack their quarterback. We needed to take out their cheerleaders and support staff. We needed to—

I stopped, having exhausted my knowledge of football. If I got stuck, I could always call Tank and ask for more metaphors.

In the mean time—I gathered up the scribbled pages of notes on the table—I would get back to work and look for something to help us turn this game around.

They all came looking for me. Usually we rendezvous in Chad's room since he—naturally—chose the largest suite for himself, but when I didn't show up for breakfast they knocked on my door. I stumbled through the foyer, threw the door open, and trudged back to the dining room table, which I had covered in calculations and notes.

"What's all this stuff?" Brenda set a cup of chai tea and a bagel next to my laptop. "And what's up with the baggage under the eyes, girl? You look like you've been sitting here all night."

"I have." I drew a deep breath and pinched the bridge of my nose. "Thanks for reminding me."

I leaned back and yawned as Tank, Daniel, and Chad trooped into the room. Chad stopped in the kitchen and crinkled up his nose. "Whoa. Smells like garbage in here."

"It *is* garbage—hasn't been emptied in a while." I pushed away from the table. "Sorry about that, but I've been hanging out the 'do not disturb sign.' I'm terrified the maid will throw out my research notes while she's cleaning up."

Brenda arched a brow. "That's what you call this mess? Research?"

I shrugged and reached for the chai. "Those piles might be messy, but I know what's in every pile."

Chad dropped into the easy chair, grabbed the remote, and powered on the TV. "Did you see? The news about Beijing has hit every network. Apparently, a group of armed terrorists attempted to assassinate Ambrosi Giacomo, and only the quick thinking of the Chinese forces saved his life."

"Is that what they're saying?" I swiveled in my chair and leaned forward to watch.

We all sat silently as a reporter from *Good Morning America* spoke over blurry video footage from two days earlier in China. We saw Giacomo go down, then we saw Tank run up and bend over the fallen man. Except the footage didn't show Tank, it showed some big Asian guy in black.

"How'd they do that?" Brenda asked. "I've heard of photoshopping pictures, but this is—"

"Duh." Chad looked at Brenda as if she were an idiot. "If they can alter pictures, they can alter video. Video is nothing but a group of fast-moving images."

Brenda glared at him. "Don't you need a license to be that rude?"

ANGELA HUNT

Uh oh. She fired the first salvo, which meant the second was on its way.

Chad didn't disappoint. "Keep talking, smart mouth. Someday you'll say something intelligent."

"Hey!" Daniel frowned at Chad. "Don't be mean to my mom."

"It's okay, sweetie." Brenda ran her fingers through Daniel's brown hair. "Just think of Chad as a water bug on the surface of life."

I sighed and turned away from the TV. Not even nine a.m., and the insult championships had already begun.

"By the way—" Chad swiveled to look at me— "if it were a real championship, you know I'd win."

"Chad," I warned, my temper rising. "Stop reading my mind. It's invasive."

"You're cute when you're angry." He waggled his brows at me, then turned his attention to Tank. "Speaking of water bugs, I don't think we've officially debriefed after our Beijing mission."

Tank went the color of a Valentine rose.

"So tell me, big guy—what you were thinking when you ran up there to save the man who had just tried to kill us?"

Tank's gaze darted left, right, up, down—searching for help that wasn't coming. "I, um—"

"That's enough." I gave Chad a sharp look. "Tank did what he did because he felt he had to. Enough said."

"But—"

I held up my hand. "Don't say another word about it."

Chad drew himself up to his full height. "You're cute, Sweet Cheeks, but what gives you the right to

6

close the conversation? This is a democracy—at least I thought it was. And if we want to hold Tank accountable—"

"We don't." Brenda dipped her head in an abrupt nod. "Fish gotta swim, birds gotta fly, and all that. Leave the cowboy alone."

I looked at Brenda as if an alien had taken over her body.

She caught my gaze and shook her head. "Yeah, yeah, I know it sounds like I'm goin' soft. But though Cowboy may not be the brightest bulb in the pack, at least he shines, right?"

I smiled. "Yeah. That he does."

I loved that about him.

Chapter 2

An hour later we were still slumped in our places, more depressed than ever because I had dropped Brenda's last sketch onto the coffee table. The sight of our dead, scattered bodies around an ominous figure wasn't exactly a pick-me-up, and none of us were sure what it meant.

Except Tank. He took one look, then leaned forward and folded his hands. "I know what it means," he said, his eyes serious. "It means, 'There is no greater love than to lay down one's life for one's friends.'"

Brenda wasn't exactly thrilled by Tank's interpretation. "You're makin' no sense." She pointed to the figure that most closely resembled her. "I didn't die in Beijing, and neither did you. And neither, I must remind you, did Ambrosi freakin' Giacomo."

Tank ignored her not-so-subtle barb. "But we were ready to die, weren't we? I mean, when the bullets started flying I knew they were trying to get to Daniel. I didn't know why, but—"

"Because his gift is the strongest." I looked at our youngest team member and smiled. "Because he sees what other people can't. Because he can see the reality of the supernatural world, he can see right through all those fake peace-talking world leaders."

"He's also the youngest." Chad leaned forward. "I mean, we're not exactly old, but we've got fifteen, twenty years on him. Assuming Daniel is able to live a normal lifespan, he'll be around longer than the rest of us. He'll have more time to do damage."

"I think they want Daniel most because he's an innocent. They want to destroy his faith." Brenda's words came out as a hoarse whisper, as if forced through a tight throat. "Doesn't evil love to spoil innocence? That's—that's what happened to me as a kid. An uncle." Tears welled in her eyes and spilled onto her cheeks as she shifted her gaze to the empty wall behind the sofa. "And when it was all over, I knew I would never trust anyone again."

We sat perfectly still as the full meaning of her words took hold. I'm not sure how much Daniel could read between the lines, but I got up and sat beside Brenda so I could hug her.

After a long minute, Chad slapped his thighs and stood. "Got anything to drink in your fridge, Red?"

"Diet Coke." I pushed the words past the lump that lingered in my throat.

Chad was halfway to the kitchenette when a knock came from the door. He looked at me. "Expecting someone? Room service, maybe?"

I shook my head, and Chad laughed. "Maybe the housekeeper wants to speak to you about that mess on the table."

I gave Brenda a final hug and stood as he opened the door. I glanced toward the entry, half-hoping someone had thought to order a decent breakfast, then I froze. "Professor? . . . You're here!"

I covered the distance to the doorway in about three steps and threw my arms around him. "How? Why? I didn't think we'd ever see you—in the flesh, I mean—but here you are, and you have to tell us how you managed it, where you've been, and why you came back, of all times to return—"

He pried my arms from his shoulders, then lifted his hands in a pose of surrender. "Hush, Andi, and I'll explain everything. I promise."

Still thunderstruck, I stepped aside so he could join the group.

Tank, Brenda, and Daniel stood when the professor entered the living room. Though their reactions weren't as over-the-top as mine, they were obviously glad to see him. "I never thought I'd say this, but I kinda missed you," Brenda said, grinning as she gave him a hug.

Daniel threw his arms around the professor's waist and got a pat on the head in return. And when the professor stuck out his hand to shake Tank's, the big guy locked the older man in a bear hug and lifted him off the floor.

"Ooof," the professor said. "Sure, Tank, glad to see you, too. Now put me down, will you?"

Tank obliged, which left the professor with only one other person to greet. Chad put out his hand and the professor shook it, smiling as he did. "Nice to see you again," the professor said. "You've been a great addition to the team."

"I had big shoes to fill," Chad said, with unusual humility. Brenda and I gave each other *what the heck?* looks as the professor and Chad sank to the sofa.

When we had all settled in the living room, the professor straightened and looked around the circle. "I have to say, it's good to be back where I belong. I don't know if you realized why I wanted to travel to another dimension, but I was at a place where I had begun to regret many of the choices I'd made in my life journey. I thought I could go to an alternate dimension, one where James McKinney made better decisions."

Tank's eyes widened. "What sort of decisions are you talkin' about?"

The professor smiled. "I went all the way back to my college years, where I decided to abandon a lovely girl so I could enter the priesthood. I thought I could correct that mistake, so I wouldn't become a priest, I wouldn't become cynical and bitter, and I wouldn't turn my back on God. I would remain the simpler, happier man I had been in my youth."

"Did it work?" Chad asked.

"Of course. I went to a dimension where time traveled more slowly and found myself in college. But in that lay the problem—I *found* myself, but I couldn't *replace* myself. I couldn't even murder my younger self and step in to take his place because he was young, and I was old. The physical effects of age, apparently, do not vanish when one travels to another dimension. Just as a turtle can go nowhere without his shell, so a human cannot travel between dimensions without his body."

"That makes sense," Tank said, nodding. "The first book in the Bible talks about how God made Adam from the dust of the earth, then breathed life, or the soul, into him. Man is made of two parts; ain't no getting around it."

The professor looked at Tank as if he were a pet that had suddenly acquired speech.

"Um, yes," he said. "I suppose you are right, Tank."

"What did you do then?" Brenda wanted to know. "If you couldn't pick up your own life, what did you do all that time you were away?"

The professor sighed. "Actually, I wasn't gone long—not according to that dimension's timeline, any way. Obviously, time passed more slowly there. When I realized my original plan was ill-conceived, I thought I would take look around and see how that world differed from the one I left. The place was—" he hesitated— "amazing. Our country was incredibly different, having never experienced a civil war."

"No Civil War? What about the slaves?" Brenda tilted her head. "Don't tell me the South was still using slaves to pick cotton."

The professor smiled. "Moot point, Brenda—slavery was never part of the country's history because the practice had never been allowed. Likewise, there had never been a world war. And there were no Indian reservations—when I asked someone about the people we call Native Americans, I was told that they had been willing to share the land and the newcomers had been grateful. The world, as far as I could see, was truly a place of peace."

"Did you see—I mean, did the people there worship God?" Tank asked, a frown line between his brows.

The professor smiled. "Don't worry, big guy, the Almighty was everywhere. Posters acknowledged his creative powers, billboards applauded his goodness, and every newscast opened with a hymn. I suppose evil must have existed in some form, but I never saw it. That was about the time I began to search for ways to communicate with you." He chuckled. "I'm not sure if I found myself missing you, or if being in such a peaceful place made me realize that I didn't belong there."

Brenda laughed. "Fish outta water, huh?"

I leaned forward and squeezed his arm. "We're glad you kept in touch. Your help has been invaluable."

"Wait." Chad's forehead furrowed. "You sent Andi a file on Ambrosi Giacomo. Did that file originate in your dimension or in ours?"

The professor smiled. "Good question—and it came from *this* world. As far as I could tell, no one like Ambrosi Giacomo exists in that other dimension."

"So how were you able to get it?"

"I found it in a Brussels office—at the World Court, of all places. By that time I was experimenting with multi-dimensional travel, the only way I could cover great distances."

"But that still doesn't explain how—"

"My dear boy, I could try to explain the principles of bending time to you, but I don't think we have enough hours in the day."

"Let me try." I gave the professor a conspiratorial glance, then grinned at Chad. "Remember when we flew to China? We crossed the International Date line going west—and we lost a day."

Chad nodded. "Yeah, so?"

"And when we flew home, we passed over the date line and got to experience October fourteenth twice—once in China, and once in Los Angeles, when we landed."

Chad nodded again, more slowly this time. "So what does that have to do with the Professor's—"

"He found a way to bend time so he could reach into our dimension and take the file—one day the file was a drawer in Brussels, and the next day it wasn't."

Chad stared at me, but I knew he wouldn't ask any other questions. He was too arrogant to admit that he didn't understand.

But truthfully, I only partially understood the concept myself. The professor had explained it to all of us right before he disappeared, and while I grasped the concept, I still wasn't sure how he did it.

But I was incredibly happy he'd come back.

Brenda elbowed Daniel. "See? Maybe time travel is what happened to all your missing socks."

Daniel laughed, and the rest of us joined in.

Now that we had direct access to the professor's considerable brain, maybe we could figure out a way to destroy the Gate once and for all.

Tank volunteered to let the professor sleep on his sofa until Chad could arrange a permanent room for him on our floor, so after our meeting, I chased everyone out of my suite, then went into the bedroom and fell face-first onto the bed. Pretty sure I was asleep before my head hit the pillow.

Didn't rest much, though, because I dreamed of all the places we had visited in our quest to stop the Gate from world domination: Puget Sound, Dicksonville, Rome, Clearwater, San Diego, Hollywood, Newland, St. Clemens, Las Vegas, Mexico City, Bagdad, and Beijing. I saw the cities marked by pushpins on a globe, then the globe began to spin and lines appeared on its surface, vertical and horizontal lines that intersected every pushpin. Longitude and latitude, latitude and longitude . . .

I sat up, suddenly wide awake. Why hadn't I thought of it before? The places were represented by numbers, and I had a knack for numbers . . .

Ten minutes later I was back at the kitchen table, my laptop open and my phone in my hand. I was using the calculator app and tapping in numbers when someone knocked at the door. "Andi?" Chad's voice. "Are you awake?"

"Come in!" I yelled, too focused to get up. "Use your master key."

The entire group poured in—Tank, Chad, Brenda, Daniel, and the professor, who was still wearing the suit he'd had on earlier. At some point, Brenda and I would have to take him shopping.

"We thought you might want to go get some dinner," Tank said as the professor pushed past him and came to stand behind me. Ordinarily it drives me crazy to have someone reading over my shoulder, but at that moment I was grateful to have another pair of eyes on my calculations. Maybe the professor could see something I'd missed.

I lowered my phone and stared at the computer screen, which was filled with a list of numbers and their averages. I waited for the professor and hoped that inter-dimensional travel hadn't addled his brain.

"What are you searching for?" he asked.

"The location of the Gate's headquarters. Chad has seen it on one of his out-of-body adventures, but all we know is that it's in a snowy location. We have no idea where it is."

"And what are these numbers?"

"Places where we've traveled," I answered. "The approximate longitude and latitude of the events we've investigated."

He leaned closer to the computer. "I see what you're doing, but I'm not sure the places are connected to each other except—perhaps—through an origination point. They are connected by *events*, however, so perhaps we should be looking at *words*, not numbers. Why don't you Google *gematria calculator*."

"Why didn't I think of that?" My fingers flew over the keys. A moment later a calculator appeared on screen, with options for viewing results in Jewish, English, or simple Gematria.

"What are you guys up to?" Chad asked, sounding both irritable and curious. "And what kind of calculator is that?"

Brenda grinned. "Keep up, dude. The professor's back."

"Gematria," the professor said as I typed *Ambrosi Giacomo* into the website text box, "assigns a numerical value to a word or name in the belief that words or phrases with the same value bear some relation to each other. Andrea has just typed the name of your latest nemesis into the search box. The calculator has given us a list of applicable words."

Everyone gathered around to look at the results.

"The value of *Ambrosi Giacomo* in Jewish Gematria is 412," I said. "And other words with the same value are *lucid dreaming*—"

"We've run into that," Brenda interrupted.

"*Sorceries*," I went on, "*Lucifer logic, an idol of Satan, sadistic madman, Morticia Addams, economic Armageddon,* and *FBI Terror.*"

"Interesting." The professor tugged on his beard. "Now—what are those other numbers you have there?"

I shrugged. "I thought there might be a pattern hidden within each location, so I tried dividing each city's latitude by its longitude—"

"Try adding the latitudes of all the event cities and multiplying the average result by 412."

I tilted my head, not following his logic, but who was I to question genius? I added up each result, divided by the number of events, and multiplied by 412.

The professor leaned over my shoulder and squinted at the result. "Now . . . write that as a latitude."

I did.

"Now enter *The Gate* into that gematria calculator and tell me the result."

I followed his instructions and caught my breath when I saw the answer. "Sixty-six."

"Not six-six-six?" Tank asked.

I shook my head. "No. Just sixty-six."

The professor smiled. "Average the longitudes of the cities, divide by sixty-six, and enter the result as a longitude."

I did, then wrote down the two strings:

66°36'12.28"S
99°43'9.91"E

The professor rubbed his hands together and grinned. "Now, take us to one of those global mapping sites."

"Google Earth," Chad suggested, positioning himself behind my other shoulder.

I brought up Google Earth, then typed in the latitude and longitude and clicked enter. Then I sat back and watched as the globe on the screen spun and tilted, revealing Antarctica, then it zoomed in again, finally settling on what looked like a hole in a mountain—

"It's the portal. The Gate's headquarters." Chad's voice brimmed with excitement. "That's what I saw when I was bi-locating, except the wind was blowing and the area was covered in snow."

Brenda squinted at the screen. "What *is* that?"

I glanced over my shoulder. She and Daniel were standing by the professor, and all of them were studying the computer screen. "Whatever that is, it looks weird," she said.

"Like an eyelid," Daniel added.

"It looks manmade." The professor tugged at his beard again. "Or alien-made. It does not look like a natural opening."

I moved my cursor around the screen, examining

the dark spot from several different angles. No matter which way I maneuvered, the opening continued to stare at us like an unblinking eye. And Daniel was right—the top, if that's what it was, appeared to be covered in a dark lid, as if it could be lifted and lowered . . .

Tank grinned. "Are we going to Antarctica?"

"Maybe, but not yet," the professor said, resting his hands on Daniel's slender shoulders. "If we're taking the battle to the Gate's home territory, we're not going in blind. First, we have to do some research. But before we do that, we're going to eat dinner."

He tapped my shoulder. "Get up, Andi, run a magic wand through that untamed mane of yours, and come with us. You need some fresh air, and we could all use a decent meal. We can talk while we're eating."

I sighed and closed my laptop, but not before taking another look at the odd opening in the surface of the Antarctic mountain. Whatever that thing was—natural stone or manmade portal—its image alone was enough to lift the hair at the back of my neck.

Chapter 3

"So how are we supposed to surprise the Gate at their own front door?" Chad said after the restaurant server brought our food. "I mean, if we get anywhere near that portal, they're going to see us coming. That's why I couldn't get closer when I was bilocating. They saw me coming and slammed the portal shut."

"We'll have to sneak in," Brenda said. She elbowed Daniel. "Pass the catsup, will ya, kiddo?"

As Daniel passed the catsup for Brenda's burger, the professor rested his elbows on the table. "I recall some very strange stories about Antarctica," he said.

"Something about an alien base beneath the ice. I used to consider those stories pure bunkum, but now . . ."

"Why not hide a base in Antarctica?" I said, cutting my salad. "After everything we've seen, I wouldn't be surprised if there were colonies of little gray men living down there. It's the perfect place from which to launch an attack. They could send out all kinds of scout ships, and Antarctica is the last place anyone would look for them."

Tank frowned. "I thought penguins were the only things living down there."

"People live there, too," Chad said. "I think there are several international research bases."

"And scientists," I added. "Seems like *National Geographic* is always running TV specials on Antarctica. They always show scientists and researchers living in little huts."

"Let's say we make it down there," Tank said, lowering his fork. "Then what? I mean, we want to stop the Gate from doing evil things, but how do we do that? You guys may hate me for sayin' this, but I can't kill anyone. I thought I could, but—"

Brenda rolled her eyes and Chad made a strangled sound in his throat. I turned to the professor. "We seem to have a problem—we're fighting for good, but good can't be evil, which makes things difficult for our side. I'm not sure I could kill anyone, either."

The professor's mouth twisted in a one-sided smile. "I don't think we'll have resort to killing. All we have to do is destroy the Gate's center of operations. If we're successful, we can set them back about fifty years. Maybe even longer."

"I'm not sure we could kill them even if we

wanted to," Chad said. "Humans, sure, we're vulnerable. But aliens? Black-eyed kids? Monsters from another dimension? Like I said, the odds of us killing them are slim. But taking out a command center?" He grinned. "Easy-peasy, with the right explosives. Best of all, their research on stuff like killer slime, living metal, and hybrid humans will be destroyed along with the Gate's headquarters. The Gate's remaining members will have to launch a major recovery effort to pick up the pieces."

The professor thumped the table. "It's settled, then. We go down, we blow up the Gate's headquarters, and we get out of there as quickly as possible. Mission accomplished."

"I'm not so sure." Brenda turned wide eyes toward me and the professor. "I'm a California girl, and I shiver when the weather is cloudy. How am I supposed to survive a trip to the south pole? And how are we supposed to blow stuff up? I'm scared to death of firecrackers."

"Cold is relative," Chad said. "You'll be wearing warm clothes and we'll have everything we need. The Watchers will make sure of that."

I looked at the professor and realized that I hadn't shown him Brenda's sketch. His body had not been among those lying on the ground, but then again, he hadn't been with us when we faced Ambrosi Giacomo.

"How do you contact the Watchers?" the professor asked.

Brenda shrugged. "Sometimes Chad sends a mental message. I don't know how it works, but it does."

Tank waved his fork in Chad's direction. "I've

been meanin' to ask you about that."

"Ask me about what?" Chad said.

"About how you open your mind. Don't you ever worry about openin' the door to the dark side? You've conjured up some pretty scary creatures."

Chad stiffened. "Such as?"

"The ghasts," Brenda said. "They were horrible. And we had never seen such a thing until you came along."

"That's right," I said. "I remember you saying that you attracted those things because you had to stay bilocated for a long time—something about how that practically put a target on your back."

Chad lifted his hands in a defensive posture. "I know what I'm doin', okay? I've been at this stuff for a long time."

Tank shook his head. "You don't know what you're messin' with, man."

"I do. And I know how to take precautions. When I don't want outside influences in my head, I listen to classical music. Or play *Words with Friends*. Anything to keep my mind occupied and the doors locked tight."

"Jesus could seal those doors for you," Tank said.

Our table went silent, and Tank's words seemed to mute even the background noise. We all knew Tank was a committed—like, capital C committed—Christian, but he had always seemed to respect our right to not believe as he did. We'd seen some pretty far out things involving Tank, and I had witnessed the power of God working through him, but the J-word . . . for some reason, that name rang alarm bells like no other name in the world.

And I had never told him about Jews and Jesus.

23

About how my people had a long and deep history that stretched back thousands of years, and we had not forgotten about the Inquisitions in which thousands of Jews were forced to become Christians or die under torture, about how Jerusalem had been ransacked by Christians who made the streets run with blood, or about modern Christians who stood on sidewalks and yelled at us as we went into synagogue, screaming that we crucified Christ. In college, I met Christians who loftily informed me that since the Jews had rejected Jesus, God had rejected the Jews, despite the eternal and unbreakable covenant HaShem made with Abraham.

Tank probably had no idea that the cross he wore around his neck evoked the same feeling of dread in me that some black people felt when they saw a Confederate flag. If he was going to talk about Jesus, I was either going to have to explain all this to him or ask him to keep quiet.

Fortunately, Chad didn't want to hear about Jesus, either. "Thank you for the news flash," he said, giving Brenda a *can you believe this?* look. "But I'll stick to my Mozart."

"Back to the Watchers," I said, happy to change the subject. "Sometimes they email our tickets, so we have that point of contact, too."

"Have you met any of them?" the professor asked.

"Not that we know."

"Well, I suggest we contact them as soon as possible to get ready for this trip. We're going to need explosives, survival gear, a guide who is trained in demolition, and suitable clothing. No one goes to Antarctica on a whim." He looked around the circle, then nodded at Chad. "Why don't you contact the

Watchers about our needs? Be sure to tell them that we are six now, not five, unless—" He looked at Brenda. "Have you given any thought to letting the boy stay behind?"

Brenda reflexively threw her arm across Daniel's chest. "I think about it all the time. But if I leave him anywhere, he'll be unprotected. No one can take care of him like I—like *we* can."

The professor nodded. "All right, then. Six of us to Antarctica, as soon as we can make preparations." He looked at Brenda. "Why don't you and Daniel search the Internet to see if you can find anything new on the Gate. I'd like to know what they've been up to lately—especially as it concerns Mr. Giacomo."

She nodded. "Okay."

"Andi, I'll need you to learn all you can about those stories no one believes. Some of them are probably true, and we can use that information. Knowledge is power, remember."

"I remember," I said.

"And Tank—"

"Whaddya want me to do?"

The professor's eyes softened as he looked at the big guy. "You believe in fasting and prayer?"

Tank grinned. "You bet I do."

"Then we'll leave that to you. We're going to need supernatural help if we're going to confront the Gate at their front door."

I leaned back against the restaurant booth and studied my mentor. The professor had changed since he'd been away—the hard edge of cynicism had crumbled, and his time in the alternate dimension seemed to have humbled him a bit. In any case, he was still my mentor and I still admired him . . . maybe more than ever.

Chapter 4

A week later, we were packed and ready to sneak down to Antarctica. The professor kept stressing the importance of our trip being kept secret—the Gate could not know we were coming.

So Chad had taken to wearing headphones and blasting classical music into his brain to prevent any supernatural eavesdroppers from reading his mind and learning about our intentions—just in case any evil forces felt inclined to wander around in his consciousness.

When Chad wasn't grooving to Mozart or Bach, he was making arrangements for our travel. First we would fly to Christchurch, New Zealand, where we would meet a guide from the U.S. Navy—and yes, Chad informed us, this naval officer would also know how to blow things up. Our naval escort would go with us as we flew to a base in Antarctica, then we would take a helicopter to the area where we had glimpsed the hidden portal.

Brenda ordered special kits for everyone, ensuring that we would all have backpacks, flashlights, glacier glasses, all-terrain lip balm, throat lozenges, waterproof sunscreen, waterproof pants, fleece hats, special insulated gloves, thermal shirts, thermal leggings, wool socks, waterproof hiking boots, and the ubiquitous red goose down parkas worn by nearly everyone who ventured to the land *way* down under.

Tank spent most of the week in his room, fasting and praying. After three days he came out to eat spare meals because the professor warned him that our expedition might prove physically taxing—fasting was one thing, starving was something else altogether. But after eating a light meal, Tank went back to his room, and I knew he was on his knees. For Tank, prayer was a serious matter.

I spent most of the week on the computer, researching all kinds of rumors about Antarctica. Some of the tales were downright silly, and those I dismissed immediately. But others had the ring of truth and eyewitness accounts to bolster the stories. I planned to share all the plausible information with the team on our way to New Zealand.

The professor wasn't around much during the week. Occasionally he'd pop in for meals or to check on our progress, but because he no longer had a cell phone, most of the time he was incommunicado. Once I asked what he'd been up to, and he said he was merely catching up with the details of his life. "Thanks, by the way," he said, "for not closing out my bank accounts. It's nice to have spending money in my pockets."

"We had a funeral," I told him, slipping an accusing note into my voice. "People *mourned* you."

"Then they should be happy to hear I'm alive and well." The professor smoothed the sleeves of a new jacket, then turned to regard himself in the mirror. "Nice fit, right? I can never tell."

"It looks fine. And I didn't have the authority to close your bank accounts, so that's why they're still around." I sighed and went back to the computer. Though I had been overjoyed to see him, that emotion had given way to irritation—for the abrupt way he left us and for an equally abrupt return. My heart couldn't handle these kinds of ups and downs.

"Andi." His voice held a note of reproof.

"Hmm?"

"I'm sorry I didn't inform you of my plans. But I knew you'd try to talk me out of it if I told you." He came closer and rested his hand on my shoulder. "Truthfully, I wasn't sure I could pull it off. But I know I left you with a mess to clean up. Thank you for doing that, and believe me when I say I'm proud of all you've accomplished while I was away. I had my doubts about this group in the beginning—I wasn't sure any of you would survive, and you have done even more than that. That's wonderful."

"We've gotten stronger," I said, turning to meet his gaze. "We had to pull together, so we did."

"Bravo." The professor planted a kiss on the top of my head, then turned and strolled toward the doorway. "I have some errands to run, so I'll catch up with you all later."

"We leave tomorrow morning," I reminded him. "The plane takes off at six."

"I'll be there." The professor twiddled his fingers over his shoulder at me, then slipped out the door.

We flew out right on time, and for the most part, our spirits were high. Tank was no longer sober and serious, but joked around with Daniel as we stood in the security line. Chad kept directing the invisible orchestra playing the classical music in his ears, and the professor seemed confident in our ability to accomplish our goal. I looked forward to the possibility of seeing penguins, plus I couldn't wait to share my research with the group.

Only Brenda seemed uneasy. When I pulled her aside to ask why, she screwed up her mouth, then lowered her head to whisper in my ear. "I've been seeing a vision—only there's nothing to sketch. I see a field of white, then it goes blue. How can anybody expect a girl to draw *that*?"

I frowned. "Is it . . . like a reception problem? The image isn't getting through?"

She snorted. "I'm not a TV. It's just . . . weird. Usually I see things clear as crystal, but not this time. And that has me worried."

I blew out a breath and turned away, leaving Brenda to worry alone. I had more than enough to worry about myself.

The Watchers had paid for our flight—which I thought was incredibly long until I realized that typical passengers had to travel over thirty-six hours to cover the same route. I suppose the Watchers had connections, because we left Dallas and arrived in Christchurch, New Zealand only twenty-two hours later. Though we had tried to sleep on the plane, we were all feeling tired and a bit dopey when we landed.

We had just claimed our baggage when a tall, red-haired man in jeans and a red parka met us by the baggage carousels. "I'm looking for Chad Thorton," he said, but he looked at me as he spoke.

My heart, which has always been partial to fellow red-heads, did a little somersault in my chest.

I smiled and pointed at Chad, but the man came forward and offered his hand to me. "I'm Lieutenant Zeke Jones," he said, his hand engulfing mine. "I'm the naval officer who will be guiding your group on your expedition."

Chad practically ripped my hand out of Zeke's. "I'm Chad Thornton," he said, lifting his chin. "Can you get the bags? I'd like to check something at the security desk."

"Chad!" I blushed at his faux pas. "You don't ask a Navy officer to carry luggage." I grabbed the handle of my own wheeled suitcase. "Lead the way, Lieutenant, and we'll follow."

"Call me Zeke."

"Okay . . . Zeke."

I wasn't sure what was happening behind me, but I was pretty sure Brenda was laughing, Chad was fuming, and the professor—well, I was happy he wasn't transporting to some other dimension.

"Here's the plan," Zeke said, taking the handle of my suitcase. "I'm going to take you to a hotel where you can catch up on sleep so you'll be fresh tomorrow morning. We'll fly to McMurdo, then take a chopper to the area you specified. We have a drill team already in place—they'll be ready to go by the time we arrive."

"A drill team?" My sleep-deprived brain couldn't parse that phrase in our current context. "Like the kind that travels with a marching band?"

Zeke laughed. "Like the kind that operates a rig designed to open up long tunnels in the earth. I'll tell you more about it once you've had a chance to rest." He glanced behind us, where the others were wearily dragging their suitcases. "Right now, all of you look a little groggy."

"Jet lag," Brenda said, dragging her suitcase with one hand and Daniel with the other. "Just lead us to our rooms, please, so we can collapse."

"Come on," Zeke said, flashing an ultra-bright smile. "Time enough tomorrow to fill you in on all the inherent risks in our adventure."

Risks? The word sparked something in my brain cells, but I was too tired to fan the flame.

Chapter 5

We slept. I don't know how long, because I had drawn the room-darkening curtains when I went to bed and when I woke up the sky was still bright. But that, I reminded myself, was because the sun didn't keep "normal" hours during an Antarctic spring.

I dressed in my thermal top and pants, then pulled on a zippered shirt made of bamboo fibers. We each had one because Brenda had sworn bamboo would keep us warm and dry.

I found the others downstairs in the lobby,

gathered around a pizza Zeke had placed on a coffee table.

"Pizza for breakfast?" I crinkled my nose. "Ugh."

"Better eat up." Zeke grinned at me. "It's lunchtime, and this might be your last opportunity for pizza until we get back."

"Okay." I took a slice, then looked around the circle. "Am I the last to arrive?"

"We were about to send Brenda upstairs to wake you," the professor said. "But I knew you'd make it down eventually. I know you're excited about this trip."

I exchanged a look with Brenda. At any other time I *would* have been excited to see icebergs and penguins, but I couldn't forget the disturbing image Brenda had sketched. Hard to get excited about a trip where you and all your friends might end up like broken toys in the snow . . .

"Hey, Red." Chad swallowed a hunk of pizza. "Aren't you supposed to fill us in on some of that Antarctica lore? I'm feeling a little blind here."

"Right." I drew a deep breath. "None of this has been substantiated, you understand. But these stories are based on actual occurrences, many of which have been documented."

"Out with it," Brenda said, slipping her arm around Daniel. "We can handle anything."

I glanced at the professor, then began. "During World War II, the Nazis created a special department called Ahnenerbe. Officially, the group was assigned to research the archaeological and cultural history of the Aryan race. Unofficially, the group was neck-deep in occult research—exploring dark powers, shamans, and spiritual rituals of the past, present, and future.

You may remember that the occult fascinated Hitler from an early age. He believed in supernatural power, and he wanted to harness and use it to further his goals."

"So why research all those old civilizations?" Brenda asked. "Or was that a cover for what was really going on?"

"Yes. Some of the Ahnenerbe researchers may have had no idea what was really on Hitler's mind. But according to the ancient *Book of Enoch*, which Hitler may have read, at the beginning of time, not long after the creation of man, two hundred angels came down to earth and lusted after human women. They had children with them, and those children grew into giants. These same angels gave men an education—one taught men to make swords, knives, and shields, and how to work the metals they found in the earth. Another taught about enchantments and root-cuttings. Another taught astrology, another the constellations, and another the knowledge of the clouds. Others taught men about the signs of the sun and the course of the moon."

"Wait a minute." Tank shook his head. "I've heard about the *Book of Enoch*, but it's not part of the Bible. I wouldn't put much faith in it."

"Maybe not," I said, "but in your Christian Bible, Jude quotes from the *Book of Enoch* and describes Enoch's words as a prophecy. So while I can't say that every word in the manuscript is inspired, it shouldn't be dismissed as mere fable, either."

"Back up," Brenda said. "I know the Bible has some kinky stuff in it, but I never heard about angels, you know, getting it on with earth women."

"Genesis six." I lifted a brow. "Some say that this

sin—and the resulting explosion of evil afterward—was why God decided to send the great flood. But we're getting away from my point—if those angels *did* teach forbidden knowledge to humans, it would explain why Hitler was so fascinated with ancient cultures. He would want to learn what they learned, and discover the knowledge that has been forgotten over the years."

"Like what?" Tank asked.

"Like how to build the pyramids," the professor said. "And the large etchings on hard soils that only form a cohesive image when viewed from the sky. Like nearly every piece of so-called 'evidence' cited to support the ancient astronauts theory. Modern man not only doesn't know how to create these things ourselves, we also don't know how ancient people managed to create them."

Brenda lifted her hand. "Hang on. What does any of this have to do with Antarctica? Or did I buy all that thermal underwear for nothin'?"

"I'm getting to that." I drew a deep breath. "Along with being interested in the occult, the Nazis were also interested in rockets and outer space. In a town called Peenemunde, they established a center for scientific research. They built underground tunnels and created a large cavern to hide their work."

Brenda folded her arms. "I'm still waitin' for the part about—"

"They were also interested in Antarctica," I said. "In 1938 the Nazis sent a team of explorers to what is known as Queen Maud Land. While mapping that territory, they reportedly discovered underground lakes and rivers, many of which had carved out caves in the ice. One of the caverns was huge, so the Nazis secretly sent in construction teams to build a compound they called 'Base 211.' Rumor has it that in this cavern they discovered abandoned alien space craft and brought the technology back to Peenemünde. After the war, Russian soldiers investigating the area discovered drawings of flying saucers among the Nazis' papers."

"Impossible." Tank shook his head. "I ain't believin' that lakes and rivers exist under all that ice."

I smiled, realizing that Tank had very good reasons for believing the rumors about flying saucers.

"Actually," the professor said, "the existence of underground lakes and rivers is established fact. Furthermore, scientists have discovered several varieties of unusual creatures living beneath the Antarctic ice—microbes and fish and giant sea spiders. As I recollect, they have uncovered lifeforms previously thought to be extinct."

I smiled at Tank's shocked expression, then decided to wrap up my report. "Well, that's the long and short of it. Antarctica is one of the few remaining places in the world yet to be thoroughly explored. The weather, as you know, is formidable, and due to high winds and frequent snow, travel can be difficult. Even though it's spring there now, we're likely to experience temperatures of eighty below."

Brenda gasped. "Girl, I didn't order enough stuff for us to survive eighty below zero." She looked at Zeke, who had listened to my report without interrupting. "Is she tellin' us the truth?"

Zeke nodded. "It can be eighty below in the sun on a summer day," he said, grinning. "And it's far colder in the winter. Not many people have what it takes to spend the winter on an Antarctic base—I've only done it once. I don't think I'll ever do it again."

"Too cold?" Chad asked.

Zeke shrugged. "Too boring. Everything is dark, the wind blows all the time, and there's not much to do besides take inventory, log equipment readings, and play Solitaire. But you know what? You adjust. You look at the weather report and think, 'Oh, only a hundred below. Not bad!'"

Brenda shuddered. "I could never get used to bein' that cold."

"Doesn't matter." Zeke stood and looked out the window. "Time for us to go."

I followed his gaze and saw a black van pulling up outside the hotel. "I gotta grab my suitcase," I said, heading toward the elevator.

"Me, too," Brenda said. "Come on, Daniel."

And we were off.

The unmarked black van took us to a Navy base, where Zeke herded us through a security line, then onto a big-bellied gray plane. I had been expecting to board a commercial flight, but we walked right through the cargo doors of a huge jet, then sat on a bench that faced assorted boxes and equipment.

"Sorry about the crowded conditions," Zeke called, hanging onto an overhead strap as he faced us. He yelled to be heard above the roar of the engines. "But this was the first plane headed to McMurdo. Don't worry, it's safe."

"What's McMurdo?" Brenda shouted.

"The American Base," Zeke yelled back. "And the largest research station on the continent. You'll find about twelve hundred people there in summer, but no pets and no kids. It's the closest thing Antarctica has to a city."

"Aren't there other bases?" I asked.

Zeke nodded. "Sure, about thirty. But most of them are so small that everyone lives and works in the same building."

As the plane taxied down the runway, I gulped and clung to the hanging strap in front of me. For a few seconds I wondered if the hulking craft would leave the ground, then the rumbling stopped and we were airborne. I wanted to look out a window, but there weren't any near me.

The brief flight was over in minutes. "We're landing," Zeke shouted down the line. "The landing strip is on an ice field, but don't worry, it's safe."

I blinked—they didn't worry about the ice melting in the summer? Especially when practically everyone on the planet was in a tizzy about global warming?

Apparently not. We landed without a hitch, then Zeke led us out the wide cargo doors.

Moving from the plane into the Antarctic air felt like someone had slapped me in the face. My first inhalation numbed my nose, and my skin felt as though it might crack into a thousand bits if I smiled. I lengthened my stride to catch up with my companions, then looked at their faces. They were shocked, too. Brenda's eyes were as round as snowballs, and Tank had icy tears on his cheeks. The professor's eyes were glassy, and his nose had begun to run, creating tiny icicles in his beard.

"Wow," was all I could say.

Zeke broke into a jog to get ahead of us, then he opened a door to a building we entered quickly. For a moment we stood in the warmth and struggled to breathe normally, then I grinned at the others. "Like a thrill ride, wasn't it?"

"If you mean getting blasted with that first breath, I would have to agree," the professor said, a smile flashing through his beard.

"I wanna go home." Brenda looked from me to the professor. "Maybe this isn't such a good idea. Maybe we weren't supposed to do this ourselves. We shoulda hired the SEALs."

"No, Mama." Daniel's quiet voice cut through Brenda's panic. "We have to stay. It's our job."

"And we're not alone," Chad said, his teeth chattering. "We have help. And friends with explosives."

We all looked at Zeke, who had peeled off his gloves. "I'm going to take you to a room that's been set aside for our use," he said. "There are some cots in there, so if you're still feeling jet lagged, now's the time to catch some zzz's. As soon as the wind dies down, we're piling into a chopper and heading out to your drilling site."

"The portal?" I asked.

Zeke lowered his voice. "We're going to infiltrate about ten clicks to the north of the coordinates you sent. Since we don't want to announce our arrival, we're going to quietly drill and descend. We'll plant the explosives and arm the detonation devices. Don't worry—our scientists have thoroughly vetted this approach. The operation should go off without a hitch."

"I got one question," Brenda said. "What's a click?"

Chad guffawed. "Everybody knows a click is one kilometer."

"I ain't everybody." Brenda picked up her suitcase.

I narrowed my gaze, uncertain about how much Zeke knew about our objective. "Are you . . . are you with the organization who arranged this trip for us? Or do you work for the Navy?"

He smiled and lowered his voice even further. "I'm in the Navy, but I'm part of a special team that cooperates with the Watchers, though if you ask me about it I'll have to deny that I've ever heard of the group. But don't worry—I'll be with you every step of the way."

"He keeps sayin' that," Brenda said. "Don't worry, don't worry—it's enough to make me worry."

Grinning, Zeke stepped backward and lifted his hands like a tour guide. "And now, if you'll come this way," he said, grinning. "We're walking, we're walking . . ."

I grabbed the handle of my suitcase and followed the man, feeling much better about our latest assignment.

We napped, though I had no idea how long because of the darkened room. But when someone's alarm rang I sat up into the glare of buzzing fluorescent lights.

"Grab your bags," Zeke said, already dressed in his red parka and gloves. "The chopper's ready to take us to the Mirny Station, near the Davis Sea. We'll drop your luggage there and then meet up with the drill team."

I blinked rapidly, trying to clear my head. "Is that another American station?"

Zeke grinned. "Russian. The place is home to one

hundred seventy people during the summer, but only about fifty people are there now. They've agreed to let us use one of their snowcats for transport to the drill site."

Daniel crinkled his nose. "Cats?"

Brenda laughed. "I think it's a car."

"More like a truck," Zeke said. "But with treads instead of wheels. Snowcats can plow through almost any terrain." He glanced around, then brought his hands together. "Everyone ready? Then let's head out. We have to leave before the wind picks up— flying in a chopper isn't much fun when it's breezy."

As I bent to pick up my suitcase, Brenda leaned toward me. "This guy has a gift for understatement, right?"

"Maybe he's trying to keep things light. Which reminds me—" I caught her gaze— "did your vision ever clear up? You said it was fuzzy."

"I said it was all white—and it still is. Kinda hard to draw a picture of white walls, white everything. But then it goes blue."

"What does that mean?"

She shook her head. "I have no idea."

Chapter 6

I had always wanted to ride in a helicopter, but my dream flight took place in a small chopper with huge, bubble-type windows where I could see everything. The helicopter Zeke led us toward was green, loud, and large enough to transport all of us, plus Zeke, the pilot, and our luggage.

I sat between Tank and the professor, too cold to move or talk until we landed about fifteen minutes after take-off. We had arrived, Zeke informed us, at Mirny Station.

The Russian base was not as large as McMurdo, but I counted at least thirty buildings, many of which were banked with snowdrifts and appeared to be unused. Zeke pointed to a dome-shaped building not far from the helipad. Someone had carved a path through the snow and cleared the front door, so we grabbed our backpacks and suitcases and double-timed toward it. I couldn't figure out how anyone got any work done in Antarctica—in the open air, I was so cold all I wanted to do was run inside the warmest building.

Tank opened the door, and Brenda and I burst through it, then drank in deep gulps of non-freezing air.

"I-I thought," Brenda said, her teeth chattering, "my lungs were gonna freeze solid. It hurts to breathe out there."

"You know the best thing about blowing up the Gate's headquarters?" I asked, dropping my suitcase. "An explosion should be warm. Maybe I'll stick around until I can feel my fingers and toes again."

"Not a good idea," Zeke said, cutting into our conversation. He smiled, which told me he recognized my comment as a joke, then he lifted his gaze and waited until Daniel, Chad, Tank, and the professor had finished stomping and gasping and making wisecracks about the cold.

While the guys settled, I looked around. The round building was unoccupied except for the seven of us, but desks and all kinds of technical equipment stood along the curved walls. Three rows of cots stood in the center of the room while fluorescent lights flickered overhead. I saw restrooms at the far side of the building, and to our right, a couple of tables served as a dining space, though I saw no kitchen. Only a freezer—why didn't they just stick stuff out in the snow? —a couple of microwave ovens, and a large coffee pot.

"If I can have everyone's attention," Zeke said, lifting his voice. "You can consider this your home away from home while we're on this mission. Before we head out to the drill site, I want everyone to dress in all the layers you have available—thermal underwear, another layer of thermal clothing, gloves, thermal socks, and parkas. Put your emergency gear— extra gloves and socks, lip gloss, paper, pen, flashlights, and sunglasses—in your backpacks. Leave anything else here in your luggage. It'll be safe here, trust me."

Chad elbowed Daniel. "Wouldn't want an abominable snow monster to get our stuff, would we?"

Daniel grinned.

"I'm going to go get the snow cat," Zeke went on. "You guys change, take advantage of the restrooms, and help yourselves to whatever snacks you can find in the pantry." He gestured to a closet near the microwave ovens. "Eat up, because there are no fast food joints in Antarctica. The plan is to get you to your site, complete the drilling, infiltrate the target, plant the explosives, arm the detonation devices, exfil the target, and leave the area . . . before detonation." He lifted a brow. "Any questions?"

"Lots," I said. "But I guess they can wait until we need to know the answers."

"Smart lady." Zeke grinned, then nodded at the group. "Back in five with your ride," he said, then he zipped up his parka, lowered his sunglasses, and left the building.

"He's cute." Brenda nodded toward the space Zeke had occupied, then gave me a smile. "Don't tell me you didn't notice. It's about time you thought about settling down and starting a family. I know at least a couple of guys who'd love to be your Mr. Right."

I blew out a breath as I unzipped my suitcase. "Who's had time to think about that stuff? I mean, I'm glad you have Daniel, but . . ."

My drifting thoughts hit a wall. A couple of days ago, wasn't I wishing I could go back to being normal? After this trip, maybe I should tell the group that though it had been a wild ride, I was done with saving the world. After all, I was still in my twenties, with lots of time ahead of me. I still had time to get married and have some kids, create a career, and enjoy a romantic relationship with a husband . . .

"Hey, Red, you want one of these foot warmers?" Chad waved a bright package of chemically-activated insoles at me. "Last call."

"Sure. Toss it over." Not exactly the kind of romance I was hoping for, but it was something.

He threw the package and I caught it, then pulled off my boot. Chad swore the things worked great because professionally athletes used them while playing in the sleet and snow. They were supposed to heat our shoes to a toasty 102 degrees, but I wasn't sure how they'd perform in subzero temperatures.

Still, even a little warmth would be better than nothing . . . wouldn't it?

The snowcat was bright red, like our parkas, and I congratulated myself for figuring out that the bright color would help rescuers find us if we were, God forbid, lost in the snow. The vehicle's long treads were caked with snow; its cab boxy. A compartment in the rear had plenty of room for passengers and their gear, though I could see why Zeke had asked us to leave nonessentials at the station. With all seven of us aboard, we wouldn't have much extra space.

Zeke helped us enter through a side door, then he stuck his head inside the rear compartment. "It's going to be a bit of a hike," he said, smiling, "so relax and snooze if you want. Not much to see on the trip, I'm afraid—just snow and ice. But don't worry—if we should get stuck, every vehicle in Antarctica is required to carry at least two survival bags with sleeping packs, warming materials, food, and a transponder. We'll be fine."

"Only two survival bags?" Brenda whispered after Zeke closed the passenger door. "Really?"

"Titanic, anyone?" Chad quipped. "Who gets the lifeboat?"

"There will be no need for such extreme measures," the professor said, looking odd in his hooded parka. With his head covered, all I could see was his beard and a top half of his face, which seemed pale and heavily lined. "We are going to succeed in our venture, and we will go home as victors."

"Because the good guys always win." Daniel grinned. "Right?"

Brenda squeezed his shoulder. "Right, kiddo."

In the driver's compartment, Zeke started the snow cat. The engine grumbled a bit, then roared to life. We swayed from side to side as the snowcat lurched forward, then Zeke eased it onto a cleared road. Soon Mirny Station shrank to a speck in the distance.

No one spoke as we traveled, mainly because the

ANGELA HUNT

roar of the snowcat would have drowned out any
attempt at conversation. But at one point, Tank
turned to Daniel and yelled, "Hey, Dan—do you see
any of those *duch* around here?"

I lifted a brow. Sometimes we forgot about the
kid's gift—he could see into the invisible world, and
while none of us could tell whether he was looking
into another dimension or at some spiritual plane,
occasionally he would tell us if he saw any *duch*—
probably demons—or *anoit*—probably angels.

Daniel glanced around the snowcat's cabin, then
peeked out the side window. "No," he told Tank.

Tank crossed his arms and frowned. I was happy
to hear that no spiritual creeps had hitched a ride on
this trip, but, knowing him, Tank had probably
hoping for a squadron of angels to ride shotgun.

The monotony of the journey, combined with the
dull roar of the engine, had a definite somnolent
effect. As we crawled over miles of ice, I studied each
member of our group: Brenda, with Daniel sleeping at
her side, his head resting on her shoulder, her dark
hand on his head; Tank, arms crossed, sitting stiffly
upright, his head bobbing with every movement of
the snowcat; Chad leaning against the side of the
vehicle, his skull thumping against a metal support
whenever the vehicle climbed a snowbank; and the
professor, whose head tilted dangerously close to
Tank's broad shoulder, but jerked upright every few
minutes.

I loved them all—more than I would have thought
possible when we first met. Though we regularly
stepped on each others' toes in the early days, by
some miracle we managed to come together. If
Brenda hadn't adopted Daniel, I think I would have.

Chad, who severely tested my patience when he arrived, brought us closer by moving us into shared space, and now I couldn't imagine beginning a day without having breakfast with Tank, Chad, Brenda, and Daniel.

I blinked tears out of my eyes. Though we had often found ourselves in danger, we had never dared so much as on this trip. Beneath our outward displays of courage, I knew we were all thinking about the risk we'd be taking in the next few hours. This time, it was all or nothing.

We had finally come up with a plan to wound the Gate, and if we were fortunate, the wound might prove to be fatal.

Chapter 7

I woke when the engine stopped. I looked up and saw that we had pulled up beside a tall white tent, an orange trailer, and a container on skids.

"Welcome to our drill site," Zeke said, glancing over his shoulder at us. "It isn't much, but it's home for the drill team."

"Wait a minute," Chad said, frowning. "I had no idea drilling would be such a big production. With all this, won't the Gate know we're coming? This is not exactly a subtle operation."

"Scientists drill in Antarctica all the time," Zeke said, pulling the keys from the ignition. "And this team has been in the area for a month. The only difference between their usual work and this special op is that trailer." He pointed to the container on skids. "That holds the special tubes and thirty-inch drill bits."

I waved to catch his attention. "Why don't you explain how this is going to work. Telling us now might save a lot of questions later."

Zeke smiled. "I was going to wait until we were inside the warm trailer, but if you want to hear it now—"

"I vote for the trailer," Chad said, unfolding his legs. "I'm feeling a little cramped, if you know what I mean."

We climbed out of the vehicle, gasped again at the impact of Antarctic air, and followed Zeke into the orange trailer. Inside the small space we found a table and a long counter loaded with computers, a microwave, and other technological equipment. A man and woman sat at the counter and nodded at us as we came in.

Zeke greeted the couple in a language I didn't understand, then turned to us. "Everybody, this is Andrew and Melina. They operate the drill for the Antarctic Exploration Program."

We smiled and nodded at them. Chad peered at Andrew's computer screen, then slid his hands into his pockets. "What sort of readings are those?" he asked.

Zeke smiled. "Andrew and Melina are Greek. Though they understand English pretty well, they don't have a lot of opportunities to speak it. You can talk to them all you want, but they're not likely to answer." Zeke walked over to a box and pulled out an assortment of packaged pastries and dried meats. "This isn't exactly healthy or fancy, but if you're hungry—"

"Thanks, man." Tank ripped open a package of Twinkies while Brenda covered Daniel's eyes.

Zeke waited for us to get settled as we pulled out chairs and sat around the table. "As I said before, this team has been drilling in this area for a while," he said. "So when we got the report from the Watchers, we simply moved the drill to this location, which is ten clicks from the portal you identified. I am confident we'll be able to drill into the underground passageways without arousing suspicion."

"How do you know there are passageways here?" I asked. "They could be anywhere, couldn't they?"

Zeke grinned. "We sent out planes with ground penetrating radar—we use it all the time to make sure the ice is strong enough to support our equipment. Again, no one would think it odd that we'd be taking measurements in this area—especially since they don't know we adjusted the signal so we could examine a deeper area than usual."

"How far down are we talkin'?" Brenda's voice squeaked. "Like twenty feet? Thirty?"

Zeke laughed. "Some of the ice over Antarctica is three miles thick. Here it's fifteen hundred feet, then there's an ice lake at least five hundred feet deep. Beneath that is soil over bedrock. In case anyone was watching, for the last week Andrew and Melina have been hauling muddy core samples out of this camp."

Chad's eyes widened. "Cool."

"The tunnels we want to investigate are fourteen hundred feet below the surface. The underground complex—and that's exactly what it is, because our radar has mapped it—is built on a hundred-foot ice shelf above the freshwater lake. It's an amazing anomaly, and I'm eager to get down there. I hope you are, too."

I glanced at Brenda, then turned to see Tank studying me. He looked worried, so I flashed him a quick smile. "We're thrilled," I said, turning my attention back to Zeke.

"Now," Zeke said, "let's get the easy stuff out of the way. Once we excavate a shaft, we're going to lower each of you in a harness. So here's the million dollar question--do any of you suffer from claustrophobia?"

I swallowed hard. I *didn't* think I had a fear of tight spaces, but I'd never really been in a tight space, so who knew?

"I'm good as long as there's light at the end of the tunnel," Brenda said, squeezing Daniel's shoulder. "And it'll help if I know my boy is with me. Make sure he goes right after me, because I can endure anything if it will keep him safe."

"No worries here," Tank said. "Spent a night locked in a car trunk when I was playing football, so I'm good."

"What?" I asked.

Tank laughed. "Long story, and not really worth tellin'."

"I have no phobias whatsoever," Chad said. "In fact, I'm probably the most emotionally stable of the team. You don't need to worry about me."

"I'll keep that in mind," Zeke said, his voice dry.

"Now comes the hard part." He bit his lip, then looked directly at Tank. "The thing is, we brought in extra-large tubes to create this shaft. We made the tubes and drill bits as wide as we could, but they're only thirty inches across. That sounded plenty big when we had them made, but looking at you—"

We all stared at Tank, whose shoulders seemed to swell as we watched. Tank had always been a big guy, but was he thirty inches wide?

"He can't be that big," I said, standing. "He's not obese."

Brenda's eyes filled with doubt. "Got a tape measure?"

I didn't have a tape measure, but Zeke pulled one from a box of stuff next to Melina's computer. "Here you go."

I took the measure from him, then hesitantly approached Tank. His face went the color of a tomato as I touched the beginning of the tape to his left shoulder.

"Who wants to bet?" Chad asked as I ran the tape across Tank's back. "I'm thinkin' the Cowboy isn't going to fit—"

"No betting," I said, feeling like a weary teacher with unruly students. "And Tank is going to fit through whatever he needs to fit through."

I touched the tape to his right shoulder and grimaced. "Thirty-three inches."

"Wait a minute." Tank hunched forward and hugged himself, bringing his arms and shoulders closer together. "I guess it's a good thing the Lord made me flexible, huh?"

I ran the tape again as Tank shrank to twenty-eight inches across. "You'll fit," I said slowly, "but I don't think it's going to be a comfortable ride."

Zeke nodded, but a line had crept between his brows. "Maybe you should sit this one out, pal."

Tank shook his head. "I go where they go. No matter what."

"He goes," Daniel said, his voice a high treble in the room. "We can't do it without him."

The professor patted Daniel's shoulder, then looked at Zeke. "I guess that settles things, doesn't it?"

I had to agree.

Zeke told us to relax as the drill team finished carving out the shaft we'd use for our descent. Brenda and Daniel went off to watch a curious seal who was crawling at the edge of the camp while Tank climbed into the snowcat. I could see him through the window, sitting alone in the cab, his head bowed and eyes closed. He was praying, and I had a pretty good idea he was asking God to let us make it out alive.

Since I had no idea what to do with myself, I joined the professor and Chad in the orange trailer. Chad was looking over Andrew's and Melina's shoulders (and probably annoying them to death), while the professor was writing on a sheet of notebook paper.

"Keeping a journal?" I asked, keeping my voice light.

The professor smiled and shifted so I couldn't see the page. "Something like that."

I dropped into a chair and stared out the wide windows. The wind had picked up, fluttering the white tent that surrounded the tall drilling rig. The wind had to be making the air feel even colder, so I doubted Brenda and Daniel would remain outside much longer.

"Cute seal," I said, watching Brenda and Daniel through the window.

Zeke grunted. "It's gonna die."

"What?"

He looked up from his tablet computer. "Happens every now and then. Somehow they get turned around, and they crawl for miles looking for the ocean. Most of them eventually die from starvation."

I stammered in disbelief. "Well—what—why don't you do something? Pick him up and turn him around!"

Zeke shook his head. "We can't. Everyone who works down here has to obey the law, and the law says we can't interfere with the wildlife. What happens, happens."

"Even though it's going to *die*?"

He nodded.

"That's terrible!"

"It is what it is."

I turned away from the distressing sight of the wayward seal. Brenda and Daniel had no idea what lay ahead for that animal, and they'd be horrified if they knew.

I looked around, frantically searching for something else to talk about. "How long does it take them to set up the drill?"

"When we're drilling into the soil, about twenty-four hours," Zeke said. "But for your gig, we don't have to drill so far. They started drilling before we arrived, so the tunnel should be ready within the hour."

I shivered, not from cold, but from the thought of dropping thousands of feet through ice. If something happened—if the cable broke, if a sudden storm toppled the drill, if we got lost in the tunnels—I would never see sunlight again. Never see trees again. Never see—

"It's go time." Zeke set his tablet on the table and stood. "The tunnel is ready, so let's round up your team."

I stood and went outside, then called Brenda and Daniel. When I turned to the snowcat, Tank was already climbing out of the vehicle.

When we were all back inside the operations trailer, Zeke was wearing a blue harness over his thermal pants. "Glad you're all here," he said, "because I wanted to demonstrate how this harness is worn. There are loops for your legs, so you step into those first and pull them up. Then you fasten this blue band around your waist and inset the tab until it clicks. Sort of like a pair of invisible shorts, right?"

"That's all it is?" Brenda asked, her eyes wide. "Just those three little bands?"

"And the cable." Zeke said. "That's the important part. You hold tight to the cable as you descend into the tunnel. Everyone clear on that?"

I looked around the circle. Brenda wore a full-on frown, and even Chad looked a tad anxious. Tank was eyeing the harness with a skeptical look, but the professor appeared completely confident.

At least one of us was.

"Now that the tunnel is complete, we have to move quickly," Zeke continued. "The ice is made up of natural layers, and the layers are in near-constant motion. The ice below is constantly being melted by the warmth of underground lake, and the ice above is affected by the sun." He held up his hands and positioned them side by side, palms down, with one slightly higher than the other. "Imagine that our tunnel is the space between my hands. We have drilled through two main layers of ice, and the tunnel is stable, for now. But the shifting of the ice layers can be abrupt, so if the top layer suddenly lurches forward—" he moved his left hand toward the right, closing the gap between his hands— "we could lose our passageway and anyone who happens to be in it."

Chad lifted his head. "Isn't there some way—I mean, can't your instruments warn us of an impending shift?"

"Sometimes," Zeke answered. "But sometimes a shift can occur without warning, like a car skidding on ice. So let's get moving."

As my head filled with visions of a moving wall of ice, I led the others out of the trailer and toward the white tent. A pair of drill operators, men we hadn't yet met, nodded at us.

Zeke brought up the rear, but moved directly to the circular hole that had been cut into the ice. Thirty inches did not seem very wide when I looked at Zeke in his puffy parka and backpack.

He hooked a carabiner that was part of his harness to another dangling from a cable. In one glance I took in the cable, a pulley, a crane, and a huge spool with metal cable wound around it. I knew nothing about drills, but it looked as though they had brought enough cable to lower us to the center of the earth.

"Here's how we're doing this," Zeke said, looking us over. "I'm going first to test the ground down there—I should land in one of the hollow chambers.

If everything's good, I'll step out of the harness and sent it back up. After me, let's have the professor, then Chad, Brenda, Daniel, and Andi. Tank—" Zeke grinned— "you'll bring up the rear. The guys here will help you into the harness and make sure everything's done properly. All right?"

We nodded. Zeke did quick check of his harness, then walked to the edge of the round opening and stepped into empty space. Instead of falling, he dangled from the crane, then he gave a thumbs up to the operators. They pushed a button and Zeke began to descend, slowly at first, then at a more rapid rate.

"Whoa," Chad murmured. "Talk about your journey to the center of the earth . . ."

I shifted my gaze to the thick cable, which kept moving, taking Zeke lower and lower and lower . . .

Finally, it stopped. I exhaled in relief, then turned to the professor, who would be going down as soon as the cable and harness returned from below.

"Are you sure you're okay with this?" I asked. "You don't have to go down there."

He smiled. "Don't be a mother hen, Andi. I'm an intrepid inter-dimensional explorer, remember?"

I tilted my head, tempted to point out that he was also older than anyone else in our group, but I didn't think he'd appreciate the observation.

When the harness came up empty, one of the crane operators caught it. The professor stepped into the blue straps that went around the legs, then stood calmly while one of the crane operators pulled it up and fastened it around his waist. They hooked the carabiners to the cable and then, like Zeke, the professor grabbed the cable and stepped into the open tunnel. He dangled, grinning, while the operators lowered him into the ice tunnel.

I shivered in a wave of self-pity. I would have to watch and wait as Chad, Brenda, and Daniel went down, then it would finally be my turn, then Tank's.

And the risk of shifting ice increased with every passing moment.

Chapter 8

"Ready?" The crane operator grinned at me when I gave him a thumbs-up. Then the crane began to whine and the white world of snow and ice inched away, replaced by a wall of blue.

Something niggled at my memory . . . white to blue. Brenda's vision! She had seen a world of white that gave way to a world of blue, so surely this is what she'd seen. Aside from my red parka, I could see nothing but blue as the walls of the hollowed out tunnel slid by.

I leaned forward to see if I could spot the others beneath me, but I could see only darkness below. I straightened and felt my stomach sway as the cable shifted. But nothing happened, and I continued to sink, inch by inch, into the ice.

The walls around me glistened in the dim light from above, and from somewhere I heard the sound of groaning. Could ice groan?

I closed my eyes and rested my head on my gloved hands. "HaShem . . . I'm not very good at this prayer thing, but if You're listening, I'm officially asking for help. I've got a bad feeling about this one."

The tunnel grew steadily darker as the light from above faded. Finally I found myself in complete darkness and unable to reach the flashlight in my back pack.

I heard the others' voices and felt something solid beneath my feet before I saw them. After finally finding my footing on the ice, Zeke unhooked the harness and sent the rig back to the surface for Tank.

I covered my eyes, nearly blinded by a sudden flash of light. "Here." I felt someone tug at my backpack, then Brenda handed me my flashlight. "It's not so scary when you can see where you are."

I clicked the power switch and shone the light around until I located the professor, Chad, Brenda, and Daniel. All safe and accounted for, so far.

Then I looked at our surroundings. We seemed to be in a tunnel, barely tall enough for us to stand in, and about twelve feet wide. I could see nothing but darkness to my left, but to the right I could see a faint and distant gleam of blue light.

"Anything interesting down here?" I asked.

The beams of four flashlights hit my face at once. "Wow," I said. "Instead of blinding each other, why don't we shine these flashlights at the walls to see if we can bounce some light around in this place."

"Good thinking," the professor said.

With each of us pointing a flashlight in a different direction, the darkness of the tunnel gave way to blue—blue ice beneath us, around us, and over us. The walls and the floor were not smooth, but scalloped, as if the passage had been formed by water that ebbed and flowed. But what was lighting that area to the right?

"Curious." I pointed to the dimly lit curve in the distance. "Someone else has a light down here."

"I noticed that," the professor said.

"And it's not one of us," Brenda whispered.

I was about to speculate on possible sources of light when the unexpected sound of electronic light sabers sent a shiver down my spine. I glanced at Daniel, certain I'd see his video game in his gloved hands, but Daniel's hands were empty.

Then Zeke muttered something under his breath. I wheeled around, abruptly remembering that Tank was still in the descent tunnel. Something bad had happened, because Zeke was no longer looking upward, but had pulled out his radio. He was staring at it, his face twisted.

I hurried over. "Is it broken?"

He shook his head. "If I use it, our transmission might be intercepted. I don't know the capabilities of the enemy."

"But what about Tank? He's in the tunnel, right?"

Zeke pressed his lips into a somber line. "The ice shifted." He shook his head. "Don't worry—as long as your guy is still in the upper layer of the tunnel, he's safe. The ground crew will pull him up and let him wait."

"What if he was in the lower layer?"

"Well . . . we know the shift didn't break the cable because he didn't fall to our level. So he was either still in the upper layer, or the cable is holding despite the ice shift."

"What—what if he was at the juncture of the two layers?"

Zeke shot me a warning glance. "I don't think you want to know."

"I do. And I'm not squeamish."

Zeke exhaled. "He'd either be crushed or cut in half. And at these temperatures, any, um, liquid evidence would freeze as soon as it hit the air."

I cringed at thought of bloody icicles. "Listen," I said. "That guy is important to us, and especially to me. We need him. It takes the entire team, you see, to get the job done."

"I'm sorry." Zeke put his radio away and turned to face me. "With the ice in a different position, not only can your guy not get *in*, but we can't get out. All we can do is wait for the crew to drill a new tunnel, which they will do when they realize what has happened."

"And that will take?"

"At least twelve hours."

When the professor pointed out that we shouldn't waste the batteries on our flashlights, we turned them off and huddled together in the darkness. None of us, not even the professor, had a clear idea of what we should do, but Zeke suggested that we stay put for at least a couple of hours. The crew would probably pull Tank up and drill a new passageway. If we didn't wander off, they'd know exactly where to find us. We might be frozen solid by the time they reached us, but at least they could recover our bodies.

"Or," Zeke said, "we can leave a homing beacon and start looking for the best places to set the charges—"

"No!" Brenda, the professor, and I spoke in unison.

"It's not that we don't trust you," I said, "it's just that we don't want to move ahead without Tank."

"And I don't think it's a good idea to talk about setting charges," Brenda said, "when we haven't found a way out of this place."

We'd been sitting in the dark for about ten minutes when I heard the sound of Brenda's sniffling. "Better staunch the tears," the professor warned. "Or you'll have a frozen face."

Though I couldn't feel my skin with gloved fingers, from the inside, my face already felt like cardboard. "Let's scoot closer together," I said. "Conserve the body warmth."

"Put Daniel at the center," Brenda said. "He deserves the best chance at survival."

I couldn't see a thing, but a second later I felt Daniel's hand touch my flannel-lined jeans. "You can sit on your mama's feet," I told him, only half-joking. "You'll keep her toes warm."

"Zeke, isn't there anything you can do?" Brenda asked. "Isn't it your job to take care of us?"

"Hey, I'm stuck down here with you," he said, a note of irritation in his voice. "So whatever happens to you, happens to me, too."

With every passing minute, the dark, cold waiting room became colder and creepier. The only light was that dim glow in the distance and the air around us was so cold each breath felt like tiny needles stabbing at our lungs. If not for our parkas, the layers of clothing, and shared body warmth, we would have become human popsicles. We still might, if help didn't arrive in time.

I kept thinking about that poor lost seal, wandering away from the life-giving ocean. Now we were the pitiful creatures who had wandered away from our native habitat. With no one to turn us around, we would die down here . . .

"Hey, Andi." Brenda's voice broke into my morose thoughts.

"Yeah?"

"Did you—" she giggled, and I wondered if fear had made her hysterical. "Are you wearing Chad's foot warmers?"

I blinked. "Yeah—I nearly forgot."

"And are your toes warm?"

"Come to think of it, they *are* warmer than the rest of me."

"I shoulda taken a pair for myself."

We fell silent again. I closed my eyes, then opened them and stared at that faint blue light. What source of light could possibly exist this far beneath the surface? No sound emanated from the darkness ahead, and all I could hear in our space was an annoying tick, tick, tick . . .

Wait—*ticking*? Had Zeke set off one of the detonation devices? Surely not. Maybe the ice beneath us was cracking.

I leapt up, suddenly terrified by the thought that our combined body heat had begun to thaw the ice we sat on. At any moment we could plunge into the underground lake below—

"What's up, Sweet Cheeks?" Chad's voice floated in the darkness. "You know something we don't?"

"I—I was afraid we were melting the ice," I stammered, flicking on my flashlight to study the place where I'd been sitting. No sign of cracking—the ice was bone dry and completely solid.

Brenda switched on her light, too, and shone it on the walls around us. "Nothing's melting over here."

"But do you hear that ticking sound? Sounds like a clock."

The professor shone his light toward Zeke. "Lieutenant? Any ideas? The sound seems to be coming from your direction."

Zeke powered on his light and shone it into the descent tunnel. "Found the answer," he said, a note of puzzlement in his voice. "Little pieces of ice seem to be falling through the passageway. Maybe . . . maybe the combined effect of our body heat and the friction of the big guy's passage melted some of the ice. Spots on the surface might have melted for an instant, but froze again on the way down—"

In that instant the ticking quickened to the rat-a-tat-tat of an old-time machine gun, and Zeke stepped back to avoid a shower of ice chips. "Impossible," he muttered. "I've seen boiling water turn to steam the moment it hits the air, so this should not be happening. Nothing in that tunnel could be hot enough to melt this—"

The rain of ice chips turned into a deluge, bouncing and scattering over the ice floor. We turned our flashlights toward the descent tunnel, and then, with all the flair of a modern Houdini, Tank dropped into view, his face red with exertion and his clothing sheathed in ice.

"Man!" he said, pushing his ice-coated hood off his forehead. "Was that ever a trip!"

Zeke ran his flashlight over Tank's body, then focused on his bare, reddened hands. "What happened to your gloves?"

Tank grinned at me. "Long story."

"So tell it. What happened up there?"

Tank shook his head. "I heard the ice move, just like you said. The cable got slammed into the ice, so I was stuck. I guess I could have been stuck there forever."

Zeke made a *hurry up* gesture. "Then what happened?"

Tank looked at us, hesitating, then peered at Zeke. "Well—sometimes I do this thing where my hands heat up. I use it to help people."

He *healed* people, actually, but I could see that Zeke wasn't going to buy that story. Tank realized it, too.

"So?"

"So I thought maybe my hands could heat up the cable—after all, metal gets hot, right? So I prayed, stuck my gloves in my pockets, and grabbed the cable. After a few minutes I felt it swing free because the ice above me had melted a little. Once the cable was free, the dudes on the crane just kept lowering me." He grinned at us. "I'm sure glad I caught up to you all. Didn't want to get left behind."

Zeke stared at Tank, disbelief etched into every line of his face.

"So what's with all these icy pebbles?" Brenda asked, shining her light on the ice chips scattered over the floor.

Tank shrugged. "I dunno. Unless I melted some

more ice on the way down."

Daniel giggled. "Icy pebbles! Sounds like a cereal."

Brenda smiled. "I guess you were one hot cowboy."

Even in the glow of my overly bright flashlight, I saw Tank flush.

"Hot or not, I'm glad to see you!" I threw my arms around his neck, then stepped back and grinned at him. "We can't do this without you."

"I'm just glad y'all were willing to bring me along—you know, after last time."

"I'm glad to see you, too," Brenda said, "but this time, stick to the mission and don't be a hero. We gotta go in, set the explosives, and get outta Dodge. As fast as possible."

"That might be a problem," Zeke said, pointing to the tunnel Tank had just vacated. "The cable is down here with us, but now the first layer section is somewhere off to the east. The little opening that freed the cable can't be large enough for us to slide through."

I looked around the circle. The professor, Chad, and Zeke appeared to be pondering the problem, but Brenda was holding Daniel tight.

"I know," Chad finally said. "Instead of sneaking out, let's find the portal and go out the front door."

I gaped at him. "And how are we supposed to do that?"

He shrugged. "I'm sure we'll figure it out when the time comes."

"That's exactly my point," I argued. "When the time comes, we'll be running for our lives. We won't have time to stop and figure out an escape route."

"Nobody panic." Zeke held up a reassuring hand.

"When it's time to go, we'll come back here and I'll radio the coordinates to the control center. They'll have to drill a new tunnel through the first layer, but we can give the detonators a twelve-hour lead time. Twelve hours should be long enough for us to get out."

"Can't you do some kind of manual detonation?" Chad asked. "Wait until we *know* we're all safely out?"

Zeke shook his head. "Radio waves won't pass through ice. I can send a signal through the tunnel because it'll be passing through air. But I can only trigger the explosives with a timer."

"Can't we get moving?" I rubbed my hands together in an effort to stay warm. "I'm not sure how long we can stay down here without freezing."

"Wait a minute." Brenda held up a hand. "Are you sure we can find our way back to this spot?"

"I'm sure," Zeke said. "Homing beacon, remember?"

Brenda frowned. "Don't that work on radio waves?"

"They can pass through air." Zeke twirled his finger in a circle, emphasizing the air around us. "We'll be okay. When we find our way back, I'll radio for help and control will have a team standing by to pick us up." A shadow passed over his face. "As long as the weather is good. If the wind speed increases, we'd better have a plan B."

"Plan B should be 'duck and cover,'" Chad said, frowning. "Or 'hide and scatter.'"

"Ain't nobody scatterin'," Brenda said, taking Daniel's hand. "We'd never find each other in this place."

Chad glanced around the circle, then looked at me.

"Maybe we should use a buddy system since we're walking around in the dark. Sweet Cheeks, whaddya say?"

"I'll walk with Tank." I stepped to the big guy's side. "Just to make sure he keeps his gloves on." I looked up and saw that Tank's eyes had gone soft. "Can't have you getting frostbite on this mission."

Chad shook his head, then pointed to Zeke. "You bring up the rear, and I'll be the point man. Nobody else around here seems to know what they're doing. Let's go."

I glanced at the professor, who met my gaze and shrugged. Because we could think of no better alternative, we followed Chad toward the distant blue light, our flashlights dancing over the ice as we walked through the frozen tunnel.

Chapter 9

The dim blue light we had glimpsed in the tunnel proved to be the entrance to a chamber filled with objects I never would have expected to find at the bottom of the earth: Art. Statuary. Jewelry in velvet-lined cases. We crossed the cavernous room slowly, staring in stunned silence at what looked like priceless treasures, then Chad uttered a single word: "Nazis."

I spun toward him. "What?"

He spread his hands, indicating the objects around us. "The Nazis stole all kinds of art from the wealthy Jews of Europe."

"I know—but how did it get here?"

"This is not all of it," the professor said, his wide eyes scanning the chamber, "but it is an impressive amount. To think that it has been sitting here for more than seventy years . . ."

"Wow." Brenda paused at a painting that looked like a Monet. "Whoever did this sure knew how to paint."

Zeke paid little attention to the art. When I glanced his way, he was studying the domed ice high above our heads. "Imagine that," he said, speaking to no one in particular. "An ice ceiling that reflects light."

"But what is the light source?" the professor asked.

Zeke shook his head. "I don't see one. But clearly there's something."

"Some deep sea creatures create their own light," the professor said. "But we are the only living creatures in this place."

"Maybe," Zeke said. "We don't really know, do we? Someone had to create this. Someone transported these things and placed them here."

Tank slapped his hand to the side of his head. "Now I remember! Back when we were looking for the Spear of Destiny, the professor said something about the spear being hidden in Antarctica."

"It was here," the professor said. "As you know, it has been moved."

I cleared my throat. "I know you'd all like to explore, but we came here to find the heart of this place and set the you-know-whats. So we'd better get moving, and not spend all our time in what is obviously a storage room."

"But *what* storage," the professor said, slowly leading us toward an opening on the other side of the room. "The sale of just one of these treasures could fund all kinds of activities for the Gate. No wonder they've never seemed to lack for resources."

We followed the professor into yet another room, and this one stole our breath as well. The items in this room were not particularly beautiful, however—unless you find beauty in a weapon. In carefully-arranged heaps, we saw every imaginable kind of weapon, including some I'd never seen before. Cross-bows, too, with razor-tipped arrows. Rocket launchers and long missiles and camouflaged objects I couldn't even imagine in use . . .

Brenda drew Daniel closer. "This is creepy."

"Cover his eyes," I said. "Kids shouldn't even know about this stuff."

Zeke let out a low whistle. "This could be a museum of weaponry. They've got stuff from World War I forward, including some stealth weapons that should be available only to the SEALS and Delta Force."

"Good to know," Chad quipped, his voice dry, "that apparently they have agents in the American armed forces."

"Russian, too." Zeke pointed to a group of machine guns. "That's the latest incarnation of the standard AK-47. I think. Hard to tell, because I've never seen that model before, but it has all the markers of the Russian automatics."

"Look over there." I pointed to a stack of orbs, the living, intelligent robotic creations we had battled on several occasions. "Look familiar?"

"How much you wanna bet there's a zoo with

those fog creatures as the star attraction?" Brenda asked. "And a lab where they create black-eyed kids?"

Tank shifted his weight. "Can we keep movin'? Bein' around all this stuff makes me uneasy."

"Duch." Daniel's high voice rang out. "They know we're here."

"We have to go." I grabbed the sleeve of Zeke's parka and dragged him toward the opening on the far side of the chamber.

"Speaking of weapons," Brenda said, following us, "anybody got anything we could use in self-defense?"

Zeke glanced over his shoulder at her. "I have a pistol."

"What happens if you shoot the floor?" Chad asked, one brow arching. "Would that crack the ice? Send this entire place into the lake?"

Zeke snorted. "If the bullet *did* crack the ice, any existing water would freeze in an instant. So we're safe as long as we—"

I froze as the space in front of us shimmered. A half dozen humanoids appeared, each of them carrying a black club of some sort, all of them staring at us.

My first instinct was to call them *humanoid* because they stood erect and had two arms and two legs, but they were taller than any human I'd ever seen, and their faces were covered with some kind of black mask that flattened their features—unless their features were naturally flat. They wore black hoods and black jumpsuits, and though I had no idea what kind of clubs they carried, I was certain those weapons could inflict major damage.

Clearly, we had been discovered . . . and the owners of this underground complex did not welcome trespassers.

As the silent humanoids herded us into a formation and marched us down another blue tunnel, I realized I had miscounted. Eight of these creatures had materialized in the weapons chamber, and now one of them marched beside each of us, leaving two to guard Zeke, who walked alone at the rear. Tank and I walked at the front, and I couldn't help noticing that the creature at Tank's side kept shifting his black gaze toward Tank as if the big guy might try something.

I blew out a breath. If only he knew that Tank would rather heal than kill . . .

We marched through a twisting maze carved from ice that bathed everything in a cerulean glow. I could find no logic in the series of twists and turns, no pattern, though I should have been the first to spot one. Nothing in this place made sense to me.

Finally we entered another huge domed chamber, but this one held very little. A single chair stood beneath the apex of the dome, and another humanoid sat in it.

Our guards marched us to the empty space before the chair, then they stepped back, leaving us to confront whoever—whatever—sat on the makeshift throne.

One thing was clear—the being who studied us was not Ambrosi Giacomo. The Italian was a man, demonically inspired, perhaps, but clearly mortal, for we had watched him die. When this being looked at us and I saw literal flames dancing in his eyes, I knew we couldn't kill him. Perhaps no one could.

The being stood, dwarfing the other humanoids

with his stature. He wore a black robe, and when he placed his hands on his hips, I counted six fingers on each hand. He wore no mask, but his face appeared human-ish, with two eyes, two ears, a mouth, nose, and those eyes . . .

The eyes marked him as a species apart.

"Seen enough?" His voice reverberated through the chamber, shivering the ice walls and echoing against the curved dome. He sat, lowering himself so we were at his eye level. He rested his elbow on the arm of the chair, then idly stroked his beard.

"I am sure you have questions," he said, his voice filling the room. "Ask, so you may know. I have always been a teacher."

The professor dared to speak first. "I am Dr. James McKinney, professor of—"

"I know who you are. I have learned everything from that one."

One of the six fingers pointed to Chad, who swallowed hard and stammered. "I—I have never—"

"When you open your mind to outsiders, you open your mind to all of us," the creature said. "And you have always been eager to share your thoughts. I know about Smartmouth—" he pointed to Brenda— "the kid—" Daniel— "and the troll." The finger pointed at Tank. "I know about the one you call Sweet Cheeks—" the finger moved in my direction, "and this soldier, who has aroused your jealousy." The creature gave Zeke a perfunctory smile, then shifted his attention back to Chad. "I know what you came here to do, and I will not allow you to destroy my palace. I have dwelt here more than six thousand years, and I will remain here until the time is right. Then I will emerge and help my lord create the kingdom he has long desired."

I glanced at Tank, hoping he could shed some light on the enigma before us. Were we standing before Lucifer? Or was this someone else?

Tank asked the question uppermost in my mind: "And who are you?"

"Azazel," the creature said, smiling as he settled back in his chair. "Before the great flood I taught men to make swords and knives and shields and breastplates. I taught them how to make war and how to work the metals they dug out of the earth. I taught their women how to use precious stones and powders to beautify themselves—not that women ever needed much help."

Somehow I found a shred of courage. "I know who you are," I said, my voice sounding thin and reedy in the vast space. "You were cast out of heaven."

A bushy brow rose in the molten face. "You have read the old writings? I am impressed . . . and pleased."

"I've read the old writings, too," Tank said, gripping my hand. "And I have determined to obey God and his Son, the Christ. He is all-powerful, and the world and everything in it belongs to him—not you, and not Lucifer."

Azazel leaned back in his chair and laughed, the sound crashing against my ears, the walls, the ceiling. Everything within me wanted to curl up and cower, but I couldn't when Tank held my hand.

"You are a man of God?" Azazel sat up and wiped tears of mirth from his eyes. "How rich, to find you among such company. These others have only toyed with the words of God, but you . . . you would die for

Him, I see it in your eyes."

"Yes. Yes, I would." Tank straightened, his shoulders broadening as he accepted the challenge Azazel had thrown down.

"Tank." I pitched my voice for his ears alone. "We may be able to find a way out of this. Don't play games with this—whatever he is."

If Azazel heard me, he gave no sign of it. "Let us be fair," he said, his voice rolling like thunder. "You came here to destroy my palace, so I have every right to destroy you. And this one—" he pointed to Tank— "declares himself to be a man of God, and for such sins the Almighty One demands a blood sacrifice. So I will be like God—but instead of demanding six sacrifices, I will be content with one. One of you will remain here and die for the others . . . and I will allow you to choose your sacrificial lamb."

"That's no choice at all!" Chad yelled. "We're trapped down here! How do we know you won't kill us all?"

"A simple problem, and easily solved." Azazel smiled. "I will open a portal and spit—" his lips fluttered in a *brrip* sound— "you onto the surface. I give you my word, which is far more reliable than any mortal's."

"We've done nothing to hurt you," Brenda said, lifting her chin. "Where I come from, you can't go around messin' with people who were just walking through your place—"

Azazel laughed again. "I must bring more of you humans down here—you are so amusing. The leaders of the Gate, however, are far better at knowing their place."

He stroked his chin with his thumb and forefinger,

then nodded. "Go ahead; discuss it among yourselves. Who will die for the others?"

The words fell on my ears like thunder. I had hoped Azazel was joking, or that Brenda's comment had distracted him, but the fallen angel's voice rang with finality. He meant what he said.

Slowly, the six of us formed a circle with Daniel at the center.

"There is no greater love," Tank said, his voice husky, "than to lay down one's life for one's friends. I'll do it."

Tears overflowed my eyes and formed ice crystals on my lashes as I looked at him. "No. The world needs your gift more than it needs mine. I'll stay."

"You are not going to die today, Andi," the professor said, his voice rough.

Brenda was holding so tightly to Daniel that her knuckles had whitened. "I-I can't do it," she said, her voice trembling. "I have to take care of Daniel."

"It's all right," Chad said. "Tank has already volunteered."

"No!" The agonized cry ripped at my throat, but it wasn't enough to stop Tank. He lifted his head, broadened his shoulders, and turned to face our tormentor.

The scene before us had changed during our discussion. Azazel remained on his throne, but a great crevasse had opened in the ice between us, and large wooden beams shaped like an X had appeared next to the fallen angel's chair. In a disjointed flash of memory I recalled seeing the symbol everywhere on a trip to Scotland, where it was known as St. Andrew's cross.

"Come." Azazel curled his six fingers in a gesture

of invitation. "Will it be you, Tank?"

"There is no need for this," Tank said. "God does demand payment for sin, but that payment was made when Christ—"

"I am the god of the Gate," Azazel growled. "And I am holding you accountable for this trespass against me. One of you must pay—will it be you?"

Tank stepped toward the edge of the ice. "How am I to reach you?"

A smile curled Azazel's lips. "The first to cross will be given wings."

Though I clung to his arm, Tank turned and gently pried my fingers from his elbow. He bent to kiss my cheek, then placed my hand in Chad's.

"Tank, no, please don't do this. We can think of something else, we can find another way."

Tank shook his head, then looked at Chad. "Don't let her interfere." Then he turned and stepped forward into emptiness . . . and my heart stopped.

Time seemed to stand still as I tore my hand from Chad's grip and scrambled to the edge of the crevasse. Tank had not fallen to the bottom, but had landed on a jagged ledge about twenty feet below. "Tank!" I cried, my heart pounding as if to make up for lost time. "Don't move; we'll get something to pull you up."

I heard quick breathing beside me; Zeke had crawled forward, too. I didn't know what the others were doing in that moment; all I could see, all I could think, was that the naval officer *had* to rescue Tank. I held my breath as Zeke pulled me away from the edge, then shrugged out of his backpack. While Brenda urged Tank to remain still, I asked Zeke to tell me how I could help.

"Back up a bit and screw this into the ice," he said, handing me a slender metal gadget. "Then tie this end of the rope to the opening at the top. I'm going to shimmy out there and lower the opposite end to your friend." He paused to squeeze my arm. "We've got this. Don't—"

"I know, don't worry," I said. "Got it."

The gadget in my hand looked like a gigantic screw with a handle on the end. Surely I could manage it.

My fingers trembled as I positioned the sharp end of the screw on the ice floor and began to turn it clockwise. The sharp tip bit into the ice, and though turning the handle required every ounce of my strength, I made steady progress.

Why had Tank been so trusting? Azazel was obviously a liar and we should never have trusted him. He had probably intended for Tank to fall, and now he was sitting back in his chair and enjoying the show, watching us scramble in panic while he devised some other way to torment us. Soon he would grow tired of the drama and drown us in his underground lake . . .

I turned the screw until it would not budge another centimeter, then tied the end of a climbing rope to the opening at the top of the screw. When I was certain the rope and screw were secure, I turned toward the crevasse.

Zeke lay flat on his belly at the edge of the cliff, where he was feeding the rope to Tank. "It's a good thing you're still wearing that harness," Zeke called, and the optimism in his voice gave me hope. "Just slide the rope through the carabiners at your waist, then tie it in a Munter Mule."

"A *what*?" Tank said, his voice weaker than I had

ever heard it.

"Tie the strongest square knot you can manage and hold onto the rope. Here we go."

I edged forward and locked my arms around Zeke's waist, adding my strength to his. Someone grabbed ahold of me, probably the professor or Brenda or Chad. I heard huffing and groaning and screaming as we strained together, our feet slipping on the ice, our arms and muscles taxed to the extreme as we hauled Tank up and over the ledge.

Once Tank was sitting on a solid surface, apparently none the worse for wear, the rest of us sank to the ice and gasped for breath. With eyes only for Tank, I crawled to his side and threw my arms around him.

"This creature not going to beat us," I whispered with all the fierceness I could muster. "After all, he's not God."

"You got that right," Tank answered, grinning. "And greater is He that is in me—"

A blood-curdling scream shattered my concentration. I looked behind us and saw Brenda holding Daniel's shoulders, burying his face in her parka, shielding him from—what?

I looked across the crevasse and saw Azazel on his throne, his chin resting on his hand, an amused smile on his lips. "He jumped first," Azazel said. "Before the other one."

On the cross—naked, bloody, and flayed like St. Andrew, hung the professor.

Chapter 10

When I was eight years old, my grandparents came into my bedroom, shook me awake, and gently told me that my best friend from school, the girl I was supposed to play with the next day, had died. "A car wreck," Safta said, her hands worrying the blanket that covered me. "A drunk driver ran a red light. Oh, Andi. My poor girl!"

She burst into tears and Sabba squeezed her shoulders as tears streamed down his face.

I sat up and watched them, but I did not cry. Yet

grief imprinted the details of that moment on my brain: the sight of my grandmother's spotted hands, the way my grandfather's wet cheeks gleamed in the glow of my night light, and the faint blue flowers on the blanket.

Standing on the ice, I knew I would never forget the smirk on Azazel's face, the professor's glassy eyes, or the thin outline of his body on the cross. *At least he died quickly,* some analytical part of my brain informed me. *Probably exsanguination.*

Then . . . nothing.

Somehow I ended up in Tank's arms as we hurried through the tunnels. Zeke jogged in front of us, leading the way, and Brenda sobbed behind us. I looked over Tank's shoulder and saw Chad carrying Daniel, who was wide-eyed, slack-jawed, and as pale as death.

I closed my eyes and saw the scene again—the cross, the professor's eyes, his fingers curled over the iron that pierced his palms and his feet, the icy blood steaming in the blue light. And Azazel, slumped casually in his chair, his chest rising and falling as he laughed—

He jumped first.

How had I missed it? I had been so focused on Tank that I hadn't even glanced in the professor's direction. But he had given his life for me, for all of us, and now we were running, not so much for our lives, but to be as far as possible from that unspeakable horror.

"Daniel?" Tank stopped and turned. "Daniel, are they still behind us?"

Brenda sobbed when her boy didn't respond. "Come on, honey," she cried, squeezing his arm.

"Snap out of it and look around for us, okay?"

Nothing.

"What's wrong with him?" Chad asked, his eyes wide. "Is he under some kind of spell?"

"He used to have—have these fits when he first—first joined us," Brenda said, forcing the words out. "He would—check out."

"It's okay; I got this." Chad focused on the boy in his arms, then closed his eyes. I had no idea what he was doing, but I knew that he and Daniel frequently engaged in some sort of mind meld. Somehow they communicated with their thoughts, often when their bodies were miles apart . . .

I can't explain how or why, but after a moment color returned to Daniel's face. Then Chad opened his eyes and gave Brenda a reassuring smile. "It's okay," he said. "He's coming back."

"Where—where'd he go?"

"Someplace safe." Chad turned from Brenda and looked at the boy in his arms. "Hey, Daniel. Did you hear the one about the chicken crossing the road?"

Daniel's eyelids fluttered, then his gaze shifted to Chad's face. "Wh-what?"

"Why'd the chicken cross the road?"

"To get—" Daniel hesitated. "To get to the other side?"

"Right! Now, why did the horse cross the road?"

Daniel blinked again. "I dunno."

"Because the chicken needed a day off!"

A flicker of a smile crossed Daniel's face, and Tank seized his opportunity. "Hey, Dan-my-man—see any of those duch things around here?"

Daniel peered over Chad's shoulder, then looked back at Tank and nodded. "Yeah."

"Darn."

Brenda held out her arms. "Give me my boy. Now."

While Chad gave Daniel to Brenda, I tugged on the collar of Tank's parka. "Hey, big guy?"

"Yeah?"

"You can put me down now."

He blinked. "Are you sure? You didn't look so good back there—"

"I wasn't . . . good. But I can walk. And you're going to need your energy."

I don't know who taught Chad to distract distressed patients through jokes, but the chicken and the horse brought sharpness back to a world that had gone fuzzy. I shoved the ghastly images out of my mind—for a while, at least. I'd deal with that trauma later, as would Daniel. But first we needed to focus on getting out of this place.

Tank gently placed me back on my feet, then he turned to Zeke. "I think we should keep moving toward our entry tunnel."

"There's no sense in running," I said, dismayed to hear a quaver in my voice. "Those entities are shadowing us and we can't outrun them. We can't hide from them."

Brenda turned watery eyes toward me. "Then what do we do?"

"We banish them." Tank stepped forward and turned a hard stare on Chad. "Sorry, man, but you're the magnet."

"What?" Chad took a step backward, as if he were afraid Tank might hit him.

"It's you," Tank repeated, poking Chad's forehead. "It's all those open doors in your consciousness. You said it yourself—you opened the door to them and they made themselves at home and left the porch light on. They can find you anywhere."

Chad shifted his weight, then glanced at Daniel. "Okay, then. I guess I need to put in my earbuds and crank up some—"

"No." Tank's voice rang with steel. "You need to call on Jesus. Only He has the power to shut the doors and banish the outsiders. It has to be your decision, but you need to make it now. Or they'll follow us no matter where we go."

Chad looked from Tank to me, then he glanced at Brenda. "Nothing like a forced conversion, is there?"

"Come on, man." Tank's voice gentled. "You're so close. You've been thinking about it for weeks, but something's holding you back. What is it?"

Chad took a deep, noisy breath. "Nothing. There's nothing."

"Oh, there's something." The beginnings of a smile lifting the corners of Tank's mouth. "And it's something personal. Something, maybe, you need to give up."

Chad pressed his lips together, then glanced over his shoulder as if he, too, could see the evil duch hovering in the gloom. "If I do what you're suggesting," he said, "I may not be able to help you guys. I'll lose my gift."

"God's gifts can never be taken away," Tank said. "But you need to decide—now—whether you would rather be a living child of God with a prophetic gift or a dead mind reader."

Chad closed his eyes for a moment, then Daniel tugged on Chad's parka. "They're coming closer."

"Jesus!" Chad whispered, his voice breaking as he

lowered his head. "Jesus, I can't do it. I need You to shut them out."

We waited, the silence stretching as we looked into the dark passageway behind us. I heard nothing.

Tank moved forward until he stood next to Chad, then he lifted his hands and faced the yawning space behind us. "In the name of Jesus Christ, I command you to be gone," he said, smiling with unusual confidence. "Scat, scoot, skedaddle, and don't come back."

I listened for evidence of supernatural flight, but heard only the soft sounds of our panicked breathing.

"Daniel," Brenda said, looking down at her son. "What do you see?"

Daniel peeked around his mother, his gaze darting up, down, left and right. "Nothing," he finally said. "No duch."

"Will they come after us?" Brenda looked to Tank. "Do you think they'll come back?"

Tank looked at Chad as if seeking an answer there, then he shook his head. "Why would they? Azazel got his blood sacrifice. Before, they were probably trying to keep an eye on us."

I exhaled in relief, then turned to Zeke. "Do you think your radio will work here?" I asked.

"It will work at the entry tunnel," he said, flashing me a quick smile. "So let's get moving and find it."

"Right."

We started walking. The sound of our footsteps echoed in the emptiness, accompanied by faint groans and vibrations from the ice.

A lump rose in my throat as I recalled the last time we had been at the tunnel—the professor had been with us, shivering like a dog and complaining that he was too old for such ventures.

But he would have never let us leave him behind.

I began to cry, thinking of our tremendous loss, and Tank slipped a comforting arm around me. "I know," he said. "Who knew the old guy had so much love in him?"

"And courage." An unexpected bark of laughter burst out of me. "I mean, who would have thought he'd volunteer for *that*?"

Daniel tugged on the bottom of my parka. "It's okay, Andi. The professor's okay."

"We know he is, honey," Brenda said. "But he's dead and we're gonna miss the old guy. We won't see him anymore, so we'll be sad for a while—"

"But I *did* see him. He waved at me, just before he walked into the shiny house."

That was enough to stop the rest of us in our tracks.

"When, Daniel?" I asked. "When did you see him?"

Daniel's wide gaze met mine. "When you were all pulling Tank up from the big ditch. I was watching the professor up there—" Daniel pointed toward the ice above our heads— "and that's when I saw him. He waved and walked into the shiny house, and I couldn't see him after that."

My eyes stung with freezing tears as I looked at Tank, then I took his hand and squeezed it.

We walked in silence for a few more minutes, then Zeke pointed toward a tunnel ahead. "Our entry point is that way. The signal is much stronger in that direction."

We followed, quickening our pace, and a few moments later our boots were crunching the ice chips that had rained down on us with Tank's arrival.

"We made it." Zeke smiled and moved to the opening of the shaft. "Just let me try to make contact . . ."

"I gotta sit." Brenda sank to the floor and pulled Daniel down beside her. Tank stood near Zeke, probably thinking he could lend a hand, while Chad and I sat, too.

"My flashlight's givin' out," Brenda said. She set her light on the floor and unzipped Daniel's backpack. "I know I put fresh batteries in here . . ."

A minute later she picked up Daniel's flashlight and shone it on a sheet of paper she held in her other hand. "Guys, look at this."

I steadied my light on the page:

To whom it may concern:
    I, James D. McKinney, being of sound mind and body, do hereby bequeath all my possessions to Daniel William Bostick . . .

I didn't need to read any more, because the professor's secretive activities in the week before our departure suddenly made sense. "He must have been busy arranging things for Daniel," I said, looking from Chad to Brenda. "I know him, and I know that's what he would do. Back in the hotel, we'll find a letter, probably witnessed by the professor's lawyer. I'm betting he's set up a trust fund for Daniel, something to make sure he won't lack for anything in the years ahead."

Pain flickered in Brenda's eyes. "How could he know he wouldn't make it back?"

"Maybe he didn't know," I said. "Maybe he planned to take that paper out of Daniel's backpack once we made it back to civilization."

"What if *we* don't make it?" Brenda whispered, her voice as faint as a breath. Her troubled gaze met mine, and I knew what occupied her thoughts.

That sketch. The one where Daniel was standing alone before a figure in a black robe, the figure we now recognized as Azazel.

INTO THE BLUE

Coming Soon . . . the final installment of the
Harbingers Series.

END GAME

ALTON GANSKY

My name is Tank and this is the story of my death.

I hate to start things off with such a bummer, but
such is life . . . or in this case, death.

To be honest, I'm not very surprised by my
demise. I've known it was coming for a long time. To
be honest again, I'm a little surprised I've lasted this
long. If you've followed my—I should say, *our*—
adventures over the last two years or so, then you
know I've been called on to jump off a high-rise
building, fight off a beast that wasn't nuthin' but fur,
claws, bloody teeth, and meanness. I've faced off with
flying orbs that meant the world no good, demonic
critters, and a dozen other unbelievable horrors, many
of which visit me in my dreams (although until now
I've refused to mention it). I've lived through about
nineteen such missions. Sometimes I come through
without so much as a scratch; other times I've nearly
bought the farm. But God has been good to me, to
us, and I spring back. In each of those impossible
cases, I've faced death with at least a spoonful of
optimism.

But not this time.

I'm stuck in a tunnel beneath the ice of the
Antarctic. I'm not alone. Sitting next to me is my
friend— Since I'm about to check out of this life, I
might as well just say it: my friend and the girl I love,

Andi Goldstein. We've never kissed, never held hands, never said the things lovers say. She has kept her distance; kept our relationship professional. I learned to live with it. But now that we've probably come to the end of the road, she has removed the barriers. She sits on the ice floor next to me. Close. She holds my arm. My dream for so long. So, very long.

Brenda is here, her head hung low, her arms wrapped around her adopted son, Daniel. Daniel is my little buddy and he may be the smartest and most powerful of us all. Looking at him now sends my heart through a meat grinder.

Chad stands off by himself muttering and pacing. He's changed in the last hour. He's a different man.

The professor is with us. *Was* with us. He had been absent for so long, but he came back. He too was a different man. I say was because I just watched him sacrifice his life for us. An honorable man to the end.

Also with us is Zeke—a navy guy. He is our guide. Boy, did he choose poorly.

At the end of the tunnel waits Azazel, an evil creature that is as old as the earth itself. Maybe older. He killed the professor. He crucified the old man and there was nothing we could do about it but run.

So here we are. Our exit iced in. There are only two choices. Sit here and die, or go back down the long ice tunnel to Azazel's domain and face off with a creature the world has not seen since before Noah's flood.

Death waits for us here.

Death waits for us there.

So, there you have it.

I do the impossible. I pull myself away from Andi and rise. My joints are stiff from the cold. We all wear the latest in cold weather gear but it can't keep us warm forever.

I cleared my throat. "This is where I usually say something encouraging. I got nuthin'." I looked down the ice tunnel. "Best I can tell, this is the end of the line for us." Those words barely made it past my lips. "But you know me. I was born without the ability to give up, so I gotta do somethin'. I don't want to die sitting on my butt." I picked up my backpack. We still have our gear and our explosives. I'm going to go back to the chamber and let Azazel know my opinion of him." I patted my pack.

Andi rose with a grunt. "I'm going with you."

"I can do it by myself." I couldn't tear my gaze from her.

She stepped close, leaned in and kissed me. My heart stopped. I couldn't breathe. I didn't care. I returned the kiss. For a long moment, I was in heaven.

She pulled away, and stroked my cheek. "I wasn't asking permission, Tank. I was informing you."

"I'm going too," Chad said. "I can't let Sweet Cheeks . . . I can't let Andi show me up. Bad for my ego."

Daniel rose.

"What do you think you're doing?" Brenda snapped.

Daniel shrugged. "There's only one way out, Mom, and Tank is gonna blow it up."

Brenda shook her head, but it lasted only a moment. There was no arguing with her boy. She pushed to her feet. "Fine. Just fine."

Zeke grabbed his backpack. "Okay, it's a party then."

That was good to see. Zeke had a special job to do, and we all knew it.

"Before we go make martyrs of ourselves, Cowboy," Brenda said. "Maybe you could, you know, say a prayer or something."

Brenda had never asked for prayer before. Ever.

So, I did.

Our pal Al is always saying that if a 100,000 word book is 99.9 percent perfect, it will still have 100 mistakes. Though we aim for 100 percent perfection, we are fallible. So if you find any typos in this book, please tell us *what* it is and send your note to hunttypos@gmail.com. (Page numbers are not helpful). Thank you!

SELECTED BOOKS BY ANGELA HUNT

Roanoke
Jamestown
Hartford
Rehoboth
Charles Towne
Magdalene
The Novelist
Uncharted
The Awakening
The Debt
The Elevator
The Face
Let Darkness Come
Unspoken
The Justice
The Note
The Immortal
The Truth Teller
The Silver Sword
The Golden Cross
The Velvet Shadow

The Emerald Isle
Dreamers
Brothers
Journey
Doesn't She Look Natural?
She Always Wore Red
She's in a Better Place
Five Miles South of Peculiar
The Fine Art of Insincerity
The Offering
Esther: Royal Beauty
Bathsheba: Reluctant Beauty
Risen
Egypt's Sister
Judah's Wife
Jerusalem's Queen

Web page: www.angelahuntbooks.com

Facebook:
https://www.facebook.com/angela.e.hunt

64041535R00061

Made in the USA
Lexington, KY
26 May 2017